THE
LOS ANGELES
REVIEW

THE LOS ANGELES REVIEW

VOLUME 23 ■ 2019

PUBLISHER / TOBI HARPER

EDITOR / KATE GALE

MANAGING EDITOR / DEIRDRE COLLINS

ASSISTANT MANAGING EDITOR / ERIC HOWARD

FICTION EDITORS / MEREDITH ALDER & AMY SATHER

ASSISTANT FICTION EDITOR / MEREDITH WESTGATE RUSSO

FLASH FICTION EDITOR / BRITTANY MCLAUGHLIN

POETRY EDITORS / BLAS FALCONER & VANDANA KHANNA

NONFICTION EDITOR / FLORENCIA RAMIREZ

TRANSLATION EDITOR / PIOTR FLORCZYK

BOOK REVIEWS EDITOR / ALYSE BENSEL

ASSISTANT BOOK REVIEWS EDITOR / DANIEL PECCHENINO

CONTRIBUTING EDITOR / SOPHIA IHLEFELD

EDITOR-AT-LARGE / RILEY MANG

PRODUCTION EDITOR / REBECCAH SANHUEZA

COPY EDITOR / BREANA GOMEZ

THE *LOS ANGELES REVIEW* IS A PUBLICATION OF RED HEN PRESS

The *Los Angeles Review* (ISSN 1543-3536) is published by Red Hen Press.
Copyright © 2019 by Red Hen Press

The *Los Angeles Review* is published annually. The editors welcome electronic submissions of fiction, nonfiction, poetry, book reviews, profiles, and interviews. Please go to www.losangeles-review.org for guidelines and reading periods. All rights revert to author on publication.

Subscription rates for individuals: US $20.00 per year. Libraries and institutions: $24.00 per year. Subscriptions outside the US add $10.00 per year for air mail. Classroom and bookstore discounts available. Remittance to be made by money order or by a check drawn on a US bank.

Visit us online at www.losangelesreview.org.

Book design by Mark E. Cull
Cover design and artwork by Caitlin Sacks
ISBN: 978-1-59709-451-1

The National Endowment for the Arts, the Los Angeles County Arts Commission, the Ahmanson Foundation, the Dwight Stuart Youth Fund, the Max Factor Family Foundation, the Pasadena Tournament of Roses Foundation, the Pasadena Arts & Culture Commission and the City of Pasadena Cultural Affairs Division, the City of Los Angeles Department of Cultural Affairs, the Audrey & Sydney Irmas Charitable Foundation, the Kinder Morgan Foundation, the Meta & George Rosenberg Foundation, the Allergan Foundation, the Riordan Foundation, Amazon Literary Partnership, and the Mara W. Breech Foundation partially support Red Hen Press.

   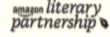

CONTENTS

POETRY

NONFICTION

TRANSLATION

TO OUR READERS
Kate Gale

In 2019 . . .

Red Hen published thirty titles of literary fiction, creative nonfiction, memoir, poetry—including a book of poetry by Erica Jong and a collection on Antarctica by Elizabeth Bradfield. Thirty beautiful books which floated out across America and the world.

There were 7,860 fires in California.

Red Hen celebrated its 25th anniversary with readings by Percival Everett, Elizabeth Bradfield, and Steve Almond.

259,823 acres of California burned.

Red Hen awarded $13,000 in book prizes to new and emerging authors.

113, 952 of us in California experienced houselessness.

Red Hen expanded our Writing in the Schools Program to include even more students who have enjoyed learning poetry from published authors, setting a new record of thousands served.

We cannot solve all of the problems of California, of the West, or of the human heart, but in the *Los Angeles Review*, we make sure we tell the stories of the sun rising over Joshua Tree and setting over the ocean; the stories of countries that don't need a wall between them; the stories of all of us reaching across oceans and rivers, across languages and gender to find our way back to the first stories, the stories of makers. We are all making meaning, finding a way down into the wild, the water, to find where the first of us made our way out of water onto land. Acres of California may have burned, but now, the plants are coming back along with rabbits, with deer, with coyotes who sing to us from the hillsides, who come for us at night.

AWARDS

ERIC CLAPTON'S GIRLFRIEND
John Mattson

Flash Fiction

Judge: Ron Koertge

There was a girl one year ahead of Brian who believed she was Eric Clapton's girlfriend. They dated briefly on the *Slowhand* tour in the showers at Pontiac Silverdome. Her name was Meredith, and she had a backstage pass given to her by her father, a waste management bigwig who had won the lucrative Silverdome contract, and so received benefits, including the chance to sacrifice one's underage children to visiting celebrities.

Brian played along with the records, but he wasn't allowed to go to out-of-town shows, especially not Eric Clapton, for whom Brian's parents reserved a special hellfire. It wasn't the music—which they hadn't heard—but the news that several thousand miles away in the London borough of Islington, a devil had spray-painted the sacrilege "Clapton is God" on a corrugated tin wall along Arvon Road N.5.

Meredith wrote many letters to Eric Clapton care of Polydor Records and he always responded with a photograph of himself with his prized guitar, Blackie, signed, "Best, E.C." Meredith taped one of these inside her locker. Brian hadn't seen it, but he had heard about it.

Word of her fame spread like a rash through East Lansing High School. The story became that Meredith and Eric Clapton were a couple. Sometimes, when boys asked her to McDonald's for lunch or to Campus Corners to buy beer, Meredith let it be known she was taken.

Meredith was not an object of ridicule. The populace did not see themselves in any way above Meredith or better than Meredith. Boys fantasized about groping her in the rec room while their parents were out. Girls dreamed of besting her, possibly with someone from Journey or Hall and Oates. Brian dreamed that Meredith played the didgeridoo on *Don Kirshner's Rock Concert,* a variety show that came on after your parents went to bed and featured lip-synched music and skits with a discoing *Papier-mache* Nixon head, or at least that's how it was in the dream. This stirred in Brian the urge to practice "Layla" in the commons outside the school library, with the hope that Meredith, walking to her locker, would hear him—and pause.

The entire town of East Lansing was complicit in Meredith's relationship. They worked her into conversations with strangers, apropos of nothing. Everyone wanted it to be true, and everyone wanted him to care about her. If only he could be in town more frequently than never. No one wanted it to be like what Brian did the summer before with the girl from the Beekman Center who dropped her pants in public. It wasn't like that. It was real. East Lansing was a groupie. And when Eric Clapton returned to the Silverdome two summers later, with Brian away at Plan B University and Meredith living in Arizona with her TA, even some parents—Brian's among them—made the two-hour pilgrimage and bought shirts for those left behind.

IN DEFENSE OF GENIUS
kwabena foli

Poetry

Judge: Douglas Manuel

The most quoted / Bible verse / told to you is / *your gift will make room for you* / no matter what church you join / after attending bible study / for a few months / they say *genius* / and mean the talented tenth / with a prophet's tongue / they say *genius* and mean Jesus / & DuBois felt cool leaving / the world / in your hands, plus you've read books / and read them still / you read them more than how to cook / for yourself / no one is disappointed in a blk man who can't eat / everyone hates a dumbass NGH though / and they're everywhere / like Family Dollar / i hear *genius* and think / they mean something / ingrown, the boy sitting / in the library reading / *The Adventures of Encyclopedia Brown* / and R.L. Stine's *Fear Street* / while his homies fight for honor / on 125th & Ada / being baptized in knuckle & bullet / which is once again / NGHs being dumb as usual / the boy sits and reads / until the library closes / and does this once / a week / for so long the staff waves at him / through the window before he / even walks in / he doesn't even pay late fees / that's the fruit of not being / baptized like his homies / i say *genius* / and don't mean smart / i say *genius* / and mean the first day / boy walks into the library / or more so, ran / earlier that day, he punched / a ViceLord / and split his lip in the middle / of class / i say *genius* and mean how / he carefully watches the clock 'til the last / second / of school to Usain Bolt himself home / i say *genius* and mean how he escaped / the trap / set for him / in the alley / because there's only so many routes / one can take to the crib / the boy ends up running / into the library, hiding / between the mystery and science section / in the far back / the boy's / heart is an engine / and dares not to peek if he was followed / i say *genius* and mean adapt / the boy reading / all the books around him / until his mama got off work / to get him / the boys on 125th & Ada / getting used to being / reborn.

A BRIEF ENCYCLOPEDIA OF MY MOTHER'S CANCER
Anna Leahy

Creative Nonfiction

Judge: Sarah Cannon

My mother takes *anastrozole* as *adjuvant therapy* to reduce her risk of recurrence of breast cancer, and it works. Her breast cancer does not return. It is impossible to know why any cancer does not recur. Or why any cancer does not occur—or does occur—in the first place.

The word *benign* comes from the Latin meaning well born. My mother was *born* with bilateral club foot. She remembers the doctor showing her mother x-rays, her *bones* on the wrong sides of her feet, her toes folding under. She remembers looking through the shoe store fluoroscope to see those bones in her feet, all mixed up even after surgeries that allowed her to walk. Her biopsies—*breast*, then, later, pancreas—were not benign. Did her childhood exposure to radiation cause my mother's cancer? The word *biopsy* comes from the Greek meaning to live and to see.

C is for so many things that it is difficult to list them all. *Cancer,* of course. *Carcinoma,* a type of cancer in which epithelial *cells* gone awry. The *chemotherapy*—a *combination* of drugs—to shrink the tumor. The *CEA* tumor marker in the blood to watch. Oncologists do not use the word *cure.* They say, *cancer-free.* Or they don't. They don't say that to us. That is not a reasonable goal.

Even before my mother gets the *diagnosis* of pancreatic cancer, she knows the prognosis. She goes over her assets, makes lists, is very matter of fact with us, her *daughters*.

My mother stops *eating* much, even before she is diagnosed. That affects the *efficacy* of *everything else,* but there's not much to be done. Still, we try to *entice* her. My friend who has colon cancer recommends the clear, fruit-flavored *Ensure.* My mother asks for the *emesis* basin—she uses this formal term for the curved, plastic bowl used to collect medical waste. Emesis refers to the process of vomiting.

Because of her club *foot*, when my mother is in the hospital for the surgery, there is a sign outside her door: *fall* risk. At first, the chemotherapy is *FOLFIRINOX*, a blend of *five* drugs. One of them is 5-FU—yes, *FU*, yes, say it aloud. My mother keeps a card on her dresser that says, *Fuck* Cancer. The nurses and all but one doctor approve. After she is discharged from the hospital, she continues chemotherapy because she wants to *finish* the whole course, because that is the plan to shrink the tumor and reduce the risk of pain in the end. After the second-to-last treatment, my mother goes into anaphylactic shock while sitting alone in a wheelchair waiting for my aunt to pick her up, and she thinks it will be *fatal,* but someone sees her struggling to breathe, and she is rushed back to the oncologist's office, where she knows she is still in danger and hopes her sister knows where to find her. When she talked about that day, her *fear* was not of dying but that she had been alone. On the day chemotherapy ends, while getting her last infusion, she writes an email but doesn't hit send—it says, I'm *free*. My sister discovers the email weeks later. Later on that last day of chemotherapy, on her way from the car, her walker leg catches on the carpet in the public *foyer* of the condo building, her home away from home. I am right behind her. I know what is happening. She falls.

From our perspective, the *gallbladder* starts all this. This bluish hollow inside my mother leads to the looking for something wrong. The surgeon removes the gallbladder. By then, we know that's not really the problem. Most of life happens *gray* areas.

Hospital, then *home,* but not really home so much as home away from home. Then, the *hallucinations* that bring her joy. Then, hospital again because she cracks her *hip* when she falls after that last chemo treatment. Then, rehabilitation and a plan to get back home. Later, *hospice* at home, but not really home, though we offer to get her there and have a plan, but she resigns herself to the comfort at hand and the floor-to-ceiling window that overlooks the city, and she never gets back to the home she didn't realize she would never see again when she left it, the home that was *hers* more than any place on earth. Then, when the end is very close, *haloperidol* under the tongue to prevent any last restlessness. Going into all this, my mother thinks, then-then-then *heaven*.

Sometimes, my mother gets dehydrated, and the *IV* fluids are a relief. I sit with her and see her perk up, and we talk for a while again. When she gets three *infections* at once, there are antibiotics in the IV too. My father had a respiratory infection in the end, so it was and was not what killed him. We know that some friends are wondering why bother treating infections when she is going to die anyway, but she is not yet so far gone that infection would be an easy way to go, not yet so far gone as my father was at the end, and the antibiotics give some energy back to her. One of the antibiotics is exorbitantly expensive and available only at a pharmacy miles away, and we know that if she were someone else, it might not be prescribed. During chemotherapy *infusions,* my mother occupies herself with her *iPad*. Weeks later, it is too heavy for her to hold.

We buy my mother a cozy bed *jacket,* something she hasn't considered since her mother wore one in the 1940s. My mother is getting smaller, running colder. By *June* and *July,* the man at the airport shuttle desk recognizes me, and the security guards at my mother's condo building nod and buzz me in. One of them had a mother who died of pancreatic cancer. It feels as if everyone has someone, though that can't be statistically true. When I think of my mother: *jury, judge, justice, jockey, jonquils, joy.*

The *kitchen* is a room she no longer visits. She always feels full. Some days, her fingers are too sensitive to hold anything cold. For a few days, she wants a fried egg, so we cook her a fried egg each day she wants one. And then, she doesn't have a taste for that anymore. We cannot *know* how tomorrow will be. Illness is less predictable than weather.

When my mother is diagnosed, she is still practicing *law*. She hands her remaining clients off to other *lawyers* she trusts. The day she calls the office and hears the message that it is closed for good, she cries. We realize that she has not been crying all along. This is a *lesson* in grief. I buy my mother a moisturizing *lipstick* that she keeps in the cloth bag that she hangs on her walker, which she sometimes forgets to use because she did not use a walker before she was sick.

When she forgets it, she *laughs* when she sees it, as if she forgot her condition for a minute and made a good joke.

Mother. Mom. Malignant. Medicare and all the ways beyond us that my mother is taken care of when that's not the case for everyone. *Metoclopramide,* to trick her stomach into making her hungry, and the one doctor who was worried about the side effects of long-term use when there would be no long term. *Mouth sores,* and the cool wash to numb and heal them. Later, *metastasis.* When I arrive for the last time, I think of myself as a baby in her arms all those years ago. I think, *Momma,* and feel my throat closing around the word.

One of the reasons my mother decides to do chemotherapy is her allergies to *narcotics.* Much of the pain cancer causes is because the tumor presses on *nerves* and other organs, and that pain is usually treated with the opioids my mother can't tolerate. One of the side effects of chemotherapy is *neuropathy,* a lessening that is nerve damage, *numbness* and tingling in the hands and feet, which increases fall risk. Another is *nausea,* but ondansetron takes the edge off, sort of, sometimes. Nausea is also a symptom of pancreatic cancer, so either way, there's not *nothing.*

My mother watches election results on the television in her room at the rehabilitation center. She sees *Obama* elected for his second term. She didn't expect a Black man to be elected president in her lifetime. This is something she is glad to have lived to see. Her *obituary* says, "She left behind a legacy of fighting for people who couldn't fight on their own."

In the hospital, not long after surgery in the spring, a specialist talks to my mother and to me together, then separately. He asks about *priorities.* He talks about *palliative* care. My mother talks about *pain* and vomiting. The word *pain* comes from the Latin meaning *punishment.*

The *question* about *quantity* and *quality* of life is more complicated than it sounds. Rarely is it a simple either/or. Often, they decline together, quantity and quality, hand in hand. My mother is okay with sacrificing quantity for quality at this point, but that's not exactly the question in the array of decisions or in what happens next.

The *risk* factors for pancreatic cancer are not well understood. My mother does not smoke, is not obese, and does not work with carcinogenic chemicals. She has no risk factors that she could have changed. Risk increases with age; when she is diagnosed, my mother is the average age of someone diagnosed with pancreatic cancer. My mother's cancer increases my risk for developing cancer.

My mother has *surgery* because the tumor looks operable on the CT scan. The surgery is supposed to last most of the day, but, after a couple of hours, we are told that the *surgeon* will *see* us. We know what this means. We *stare* at his fist, which he *says* is the *size* of the tumor. The tumor is attached to an artery, and his fist shows us how to imagine that. If it were attached to a vein, he would have tried to remove it. My mother's *sister* is there. And my sister is there, and she has to excuse herself to rush to the bathroom. In the months after the surgery, they do most of the caregiving.

T is for *tumor*, the object that is us. And for *trust*, which becomes my secret word.

Cancer is *uncontrolled* cell reproduction, too much of what's *usually* a good thing. Too many cells too fast is a tumor. My mother's tumor is *unresectable;* it won't let go. Cancer is not *unusual*; one out of every two or three people will be diagnosed with some type at some point. The way an instance of cancer plays out in a given life is *unique,* with each body and each choice and all the chances of day-to-day living. When the end is nearing, a catheter is inserted so that my mother's *urine* collects in a bag. The liquid is dark. There's not much to be had.

I agree to be the task-master about eating, showers, walking the length of the condo lobby. We all know what it means when my mother goes days without walking. Sometimes, we acquiesce with *vodka,* which we spike with Ensure as part of the bargain. Alcohol consumption risks interaction with medication; she might stop breathing. It dehydrates my mother, which makes bowel movements excruciating, and it doesn't taste or feel like it used to, which disappoints my mother. Disappointment is an ache that could easily get out of hand, so we keep adjusting. Sometimes, when we clean my mother's room, we find gummy *vitamins* under the bed. She smiles like a kid who's fooled us, who's been caught, who knows there are worse things to worry about, like *vomiting*, which there isn't all that much of in my mother's case, all things considered.

My mother is *wasting*. Wasting is not only the result of not eating. The body has changed the way it *works*, and there's no going back. No one tells us that wasting cannot be staved off, that eating cannot help much. The cause of death for my father was wasting, more than anything else. The verb *waste* may be transitive or intransitive. It can be a noun, too. It is a shape-shifter. It is the body left *wanting*. It is the body after wanting has left too.

The first person to see the tumor is an emergency room physician treating my mother for what she thinks is a gallbladder attack. He sees a shadow on the *x-ray*. He does not tell her what he is sure it is. He tells her to see a specialist right away. My mother knows from the tone of his voice that he has seen something seriously wrong inside of her. She has known for a while that something is wrong, but her fatigue was such that she knew she would be dismissed or misdiagnosed.

After doing some research, my mother aims to live a *year*. The vast majority of pancreatic cancer patients don't survive twelve months. My mother lasts about nine months, leaves before the calendar year is up, all twelves the day she dies.

After she dies, my mother's body is put into a black bag with a *zipper*. My aunt and sister are there. I have been awake all night and am too tired to watch, so I close my eyes and listen to the sound of goodbye.

HUSBANDRY
LJ Pemberton

Short Fiction

Judge: Doug Lawson

One morning I awoke as a woman. I knew I was a woman because I had seen women before. It was cold and my new body was shivering and so I stretched my new arms above my head and then walked on my new legs to the farmer's house. He was already in the far pasture, tending the sheep. I opened his door with my new fingers and enjoyed their bending grip, coiling around the knob. My bare feet tread without clicking and I went from room to room. In his bedroom I found his clothes. I put on a shirt and sweater and pants, then found socks and a pair of brown leather boots for my feet. The boots were too big, but the other items fit snugly.

A door in the bedroom led to another small room with hard basins and soft cloth. There I saw myself in the mirror and I was glad that even though I was a woman, I could still recognize my face. My horns were gone, although my eyes were that self-same dark, and my forehead broad. My body, too, had its own girth, round in the middle as I had always been, but now with breasts up top and a padded ass behind. I practiced sitting on the small basin in the room, and the seam of my pants rubbed between my legs. It felt sharp and good. I stood again and observed the pulling inward as I clenched the muscles in my new cunt. It was new, this drawing together, and I caught myself grinning as I clenched and released. My old swinging dick was gone, and in its place was this new instrument and its attendant pleasures.

I left the house and stepped in heavy thuds with my new shoes. It was warmer than when I awoke, although the early spring day still had a hint of morning chill. At the road, I used my right hand to open the gate, and marveled at the ease with which I stepped over the cattle grid. The trees were in their early budding, and daffodils sprung new from the hard ground. In places the grass was beginning to green, but the field where I had stood and stared at the sky was black with trampled earth.

Half my life had been spent in that yard—nearly seven years of waking and eating, thinking and dreaming. The siring had been intermittent and brief. The farmer always looked pleased when cows arrived to mate with me, and he seemed to enjoy talking with the other people who came with them. Of the cows: most had defeat in their eyes before I mounted them, and so our fucking embarrassed me, even as I loved it and wanted them. We were all resigned to our fates—the gates closed, the fences high. It is no good to be a bull in a pen; the sloping hills and quiet forest are always beyond the railing.

A car passed, and then a truck. Both slowed as I walked, but neither stopped to ask where I was going. I did not know, and so it was better this way. I walked past other farmhouses, so near that I was surprised the farmer had not had more visitors, and as the sun rose in the sky, I marveled at the changing light. The treeshade of the road was my shelter. My boots clapped, and I was alone. Before noon I was hungry, but I did not know what to eat or where to find it, and so I continued walking. In the early afternoon I came to a stream and drank. The water was cold and fresh. Here the rustling trees, here the jumping frog, here the rushing water. I desired the earth like I had once desired the cows and I plunged my fingers into the soft mud and grasped at the river rocks beneath. I rolled the pebbles in my hand and felt their hardness, as new to me as my hairless skin.

After an hour, I walked on. Hunger emboldened my blood, and I approached and knocked when I saw a house off the road. A strong, wind-touched woman opened the door and squinted at me as she surveyed my face. *What is it,* she said. *Are you selling something?* she asked. I told her in slow speech that I was hungry, and she asked me my name. *Taura?* I said, and she said I could come in.

Her house was warmer than the farmer's, as she had a fire in the kitchen and rugs on the floors. She sat me at a table and gave me bread and milk. I ate and then drank, and the milk was like my mother's, though thin. She did not speak. On the wall hung pictures of her with other humans: children, a man, some elderly. *Where are your people?* I asked her, and she said they had either died or moved away, and she did not think they wanted to live near the farm anymore. *Do you keep cows?* I asked her and she laughed. *Only goats and chickens*, she said. I imagined she laughed because she did not have enough land for cows, but later I learned she had a fear of large animals, and I did not know how to tell her I was once so large and so animal.

That was the first afternoon. As it passed into evening, she invited me to stay the night. The next day, finding ourselves awake before dawn, she enlisted my help in making breakfast, and although she thought it strange that I did not know how to make eggs, she taught me, and we ate in silence. It began like this, my staying there, with an hour passed and another planned, until it was a year, and she was Lydia to me, and I was home. Some days I saw the farmer in town, thumping cantaloupes at the supermarket or buying stamps to post mail. With my woman eyes I understood that he was the sort of man other women wanted to know, and with my bull heart I knew he was afraid of success and enjoyed the failures that come from wrestling poor ground. Once, I tried to get his attention to see if he recognized me, and he looked at my dark eyes for a moment and moved on. I was the woman that Lydia had taken up with, and the farmer, like the town, accepted my presence the way that one neighbor notices that another has painted the front door red.

The first time I kissed Lydia we were both covered in dirt and chicken shit. She had been fixing the coop and I had been handing her the hammer and holding the boards. It was a damp summer day where the earth and air were heavy with the recently passed rain. Her lips were tense when I kissed her, and I enjoyed their taste and the new use of my own. She put her hands to her face and touched her lips with her fingertips. *You kissed me*, she said. And I said that I had, and she said it had been a long time since anyone had done that. We picked up our tools and put them away. She went upstairs to shower, and I waited on the back porch. The once-cream paint was peeling off the wood and I noted to myself that we would have to strip and repaint it before the end of fall. When she was done showering, I went up and showered too, alone, and thought of our kiss and what might come.

A week later it was she who touched my hand in the kitchen as I was mixing the day's dough and she was shaping the morning's biscuits. We were both dusted with flour, and I remember pausing my kneading to notice the blue-brown veins of her hand. *You surprised me*, she said. *I have loved you a long time*, I said, and it was as true as if I had said, *I was not human until I met you.* She squeezed my hand in her own and the dusty flour was still as we stood there. *This is new to me*, she said, and let go. *We are new*, I said, and set the dough by the window to rise.

We did not eat together that day, passing instead into the kitchen at different times and in quiet hunger, alone. I ate her biscuits from a plate she set out for me. She ate my bread from the board on which I left it. Two weeks we were ghosts to each other, seeing only the evidence of our passing. Late that Friday I stood in my bedroom and watched her in the garden below. Her body, round and stout like my own, bent over the strawberry patch as she pulled weeds. I said nothing. I hid in my silence and waited for her words.

Her words came second. On a hot night in the darkness of my room, she slipped into my bed and kissed my woman lips with her own. *I have loved you*, she whispered. *But I was afraid*, she said. I held her hand. We cried and we slept and made love in the morning.

■ ■ ■

One morning I awoke as a bull. The slats broke in the night, but I did not notice because I have always been a heavy dreamer. Lydia rolled to me and clung to my back. Her early eyes did not yet have the day's understanding and so there was a pause between her touch and her startling. I wanted to roll to her as I have done so many other mornings. I wanted to tell her that I loved her. But my bull tongue was thick and round and had lost my woman words. I stood and bowed beside the bed and she stared and then ran from the room.

I took my bull-self downstairs and rammed the back door with my head until it came free of its hinges. The day was hot as I left the house. I passed the chicken yard and followed the road I had walked so many times with my woman legs. Again, my nose was laden. Again, my bull's cock swung with my trotting. Cars honked at me as I went towards the farmer's house, and I wept for the life I knew I no longer had.

The farmer's yard was changed. It had been some time, a number of years, but my bull mind could not quite count them now. My bull knees were old, and my joints ached as I turned into the driveway, now paved and with no cattle grid to impede my step. To the right, in the fenced yard where I had once bred with cows, a portico and table stood surrounded by flowers. My old shed was unpainted and uninhabitable, although lights hung from the roof to the portico. I walked past where I had lived and snatched at weeds with my teeth, knowing again my bullish anger. Music could be heard from the house. It was not the farmer's music—him with his swing taste and country ear. This was something else. I could not tell you, except that it was unfamiliar and sad.

With no fences to stop me, I walked to the far pasture, but there were no sheep. The land itself was divided into yards with houses and driveways where the dogs once nipped at woolen ewes. I stood in the street and stared until a car interrupted my staring. It appeared to me like a shiny headless other-animal, unfeeling and yet determined. I stamped the road. The car waited. I bowed my head. The car waited. I turned and ran into a yard and the car moved on. I knew then that I had to go back to Lydia's. The place I had learned to be a bull could not take me, and so the place I had learned to be a woman would have to. It was not that I believed Lydia owed me her love, but I hoped she at least might let me stay.

By evening, I was again in her yard. Hammering could be heard, and I assumed it was Lydia fixing the back door. I attempted one of the front stairs, but it could not hold me, and my hooves broke through. Lydia came to the front porch and stood, hammer in hand, staring at my back. I was afraid and bucked to free my front ankles. She waited. I moved finally to the grass and bent my knees and laid on the ground and hoped that I had made myself small.

Lydia waited on the porch and stared. The last light came bright through the trees and then darkened while we watched each other. She was as beautiful and strong as the day I had first kissed her. Gray, but vital. We watched each other's eyes. I snorted and stretched a hind leg to the side. My tail twitched at the flies settling on my haunches. I laid my head down. I closed my eyes. I awoke to her touch between my eyes. She traced my flat forehead and then grasped a horn. *You are a bull?* she asked. It was just as well that I could not speak. I did not know what to say. She walked slowly to the side of me and knelt in the grass. She reached and pet my belly. I turned to her and she scratched the short hair behind my left ear. *I knew,* she said. *I do not know how I knew, but I knew.*

She leaned, then, into the side of me, and I shifted to make a pillow of my girth for her. Katydids ground the silence into humming. I turned my head and nudged her draped arm with my snout. She touched my nose and I saw her see her hand beside my fur. The stillness came alive with night creatures. I settled my head on the ground. She did not stir and soon, there was a slow breathing. We slept, warm and huddled beneath the stars.

FICTION

THREE STORIES ON MONSTERS, ON GRIEVING IN THE GULF SOUTH
Adam Gnuse

CLARK CREEK

You try to keep your kids safe. You try to keep your kids safe. You try to keep them from the things that scared you most as a child, even if those things were only imaginary. I don't remember who gave me the book as a girl, but I would have never let my own kids read it, even though it had been written for children. It was one of those books that catalogues all the different monsters you'll encounter when your parents are away. Made-up things, fictions—but ones that, for whatever reason, a child's mind could obsess over. The monster that frightened me most was in the middle of the book. The Banshee.

The illustration was of an old woman with gray skin and brown rags. She was drawn hunched over, and a shawl covered all her face except the jaw, which was grotesquely unhinged and hanging down to her breasts. She was perched atop roots of a tree, as if waiting for something.

But the book said she was known most by her sound, by her scream. She was to come to you, and when she screamed—the next day you would die.

It didn't say whether she came to foretell your death or cause it. For a long time as a girl, I thought about her, that thing. I worried I would look out the windows of my parents' house to the creek and see her out there, her rags a dark blot upon the afternoon, resting on a cypress knee, looking up at me.

It's strange how these memories could return so abruptly, years later, miles away from that house by the creek where I could hardly sleep once I had read that book. When I finally heard that scream, the one the book described, I was an adult. It was the night before my Lizzie took her life, and when I heard that scream it was as though I was back, a little girl at my parents' house, again. Too afraid to go to my window to look, too afraid to even move in my bed, to breathe too deeply.

My husband snored beside me, but I heard it, and continued to hear it: that wail, like a baby's cry from the lungs of a grown woman, sounding thin through the windowpane but so close. It was in our front yard.

Eventually it stopped, but I lay awake until morning.

I've often wondered how I did nothing. What mother thinks only of herself in a moment like that? What kind of mother forgets her two children in their bedrooms down the hall?

I wonder sometimes if I was punished for it. That my daughter had been punished because of me, instead of me. Because how do we know these things are not connected? Those fears at night, ones we disregard the moment the morning light cuts through the window blinds—how do we know they're not somehow real?

We had known for some time that Lizzie was at risk. We had asked if she was thinking of hurting herself, if she had a plan. Made sure she was never home alone. We listened. She did therapy, and we talked to her friends. We took her seriously.

We found her half-submerged in the bathtub. I often think that if she could have made it a little longer, grown to be a little older, she would have realized that teenage years are things you leave behind. Now, each year is a milestone she'll never meet. She'll never graduate school, or one day have her own children. Her brother will grow into an old man and never again have his sister.

Each night is different now, though I still listen for the sound of that woman like a far-off siren. I am still scared, but I am something else, too.

I wait until I hear it, sad and ceaseless, wailing in our front yard, far from the streetlights of the road, with a canopy of trees that blots out the moonlight and stars. I wait to hear it, because I know when I do, I will stand up from my bed and leave my husband asleep. I will pass my son's bedroom and what used to be my daughter's, and I will go alone downstairs. For a short while I will listen through the front door to the sound of it, of her. And as small as I'll feel, and as big as the dark is out there, I will turn the deadbolt and throw open the door.

In that moment, I'll turn all the love I hold within me into fury. My bare feet pressing against the grass, and my arms reaching to what I can't see. I will follow the sound of that scream. And when I find it, I will make it stop.

TICKFAW ANIMAL PARK

Our zoo, near the Tickfaw swamps outside Baton Rouge, seemed half-drowned with its mud trails and weather-bent branches, with humidity dense enough to make every breath feel labored. Between rains, guests would pull back the hoods of their ponchos and wave down through the metal bars at the black bear as it lumbered to a sunny patch of straw, in hopes of drying its fur before the next, inevitable Gulf shower. My parents used to take me there as a kid.

Years later, as an employee, I still recognized many of the workers—the same ticket sellers in the leaky welcome booth, and that same old ice cream vendor who labored her cart through the zoo in knee-highs. Each of them had since gone gray as the morning fog. If anyone ever asked them, they'd say the zoo had become their second home. They'd swear they no longer even smelled it, that thick musk and moldering earth that permeated the place, as if they'd grown as accustomed to it as the animals themselves.

My first week in animal control, I learned the threat each species posed if they were to escape. They were ranked on a chart in our back office according to their danger. Venomous snakes—the cottonmouths, rattlers—were stacked below the large predators like the black bear or the mountain lion, whose entry carried an addendum on how its mind had cracked (pacing, insomnia, it had mauled a mate), as the big cats often do in small enclosures. At the top of the list were the chimps, who were smart, human-like. There were notes referencing news stories of what they'd done with their teeth and nails to handlers that had tried to treat them as pets, scolding and spanking them like children.

Escaped chimpanzees would be a crisis, it was said, but I couldn't see any of that happening from her, from Angie. Not considering how she would be when I'd find her in the mornings—still curled from sleep, on top of the concession stand outside her cage, smacking her lips and blinking down at me.

I first found her not long after I got the job, during one of those times I drove in so early it was still nearly night. I couldn't sleep, so I walked the exhibits, pacing the length of the place, listening to the garbled calls the birds made in their cages. I can't forget how strange those walks would be, with the dark obscuring the chain links of the animals' pens, with how the live oak branches seemed like massive, reaching hands. I'd hear the sound of the mountain lion's paws tramping the mud, its breath like something from a childhood nightmare. Sometimes I'd catch the glint of an animal's eyes in the dark, and I'd realize it had been watching me.

I found Angie up there dozing with her arms across her chest, lying on her side towards the pink light of the sun rising up over the canopy. From the look of her, I figured she gotten out of her pen so she could catch a spot of light to warm herself, or a breeze to dry the night's dew from her shoulders. I knew the protocol if they found out she had escaped: how they'd renovate the whole enclosure, reshape it, drape netting across the canopy. They'd keep her down in one of those damp, basement holding cages until they were done.

So, I chatted at her for a bit. I talked, with her just an arm's reach away on the awning, saying nothing in particular, until finally she rubbed her face with an open palm and hopped back along the long, overhead branches to her home. I didn't see the need to tell anyone else.

But then I'd find her out there again, on other walks, always early in the morning,

perched on that same awning, until the thing became a kind of ritual of ours. Each night, I'd go to bed early enough so I could wake up in time before the handlers came in, so I could wake Angie up outside her cage. I'd even do it on my off-days, because there was no knowing which nights she would choose to escape. But I never minded any of it.

I remember thinking, during that time, how proud I would have been as a child, standing on the exhibit railings, to know that I'd grow up to care for an ape like Angie. My job in animal control kept us in an office. We waited with our charts, with command poles, with our rifles, waiting for something to go wrong. An escape. A child falling into an exhibit. And for teeth to tear down upon the softness of a neck and face. It was nice to have something more.

All it took was one time waking up late, staring at the digits of my bedroom clock in disbelief. I raced along I-55, passing as much of the traffic along the shoulder as I could, because I knew, somehow, that even though Angie didn't go out every morning, she had that day. Because it had rained the night before. Because lately she had been coming out more. Because she liked meeting me out there, and I had never let her know that it wasn't okay.

The zoo's front gates were still closed. Inside, I found them circled around the concessions booth, around her, with their tranquillizer guns and their long, noosed command poles—one handler holding his rifle, trained up at her. Angie looked down from her perch, dazed from sleep, as if she hadn't yet realized these men weren't part of a dream.

It wasn't her fault. I don't know why I got so mad at her. She didn't know what it meant if someone else were to find her—what would happen if she wasn't careful. I wasn't thinking when I snatched a command pole from one of the handlers and looped its noose around Angie's neck.

I tightened it too much around her throat, but I tugged on Angie anyway. I forced her from the awning, making her hoot out in pain each time I yanked. I didn't think—forcing her to descend with one arm on the drainpipe, one hand pawing at the cord around her neck. Before they took the pole from me—wresting it away, loosening it so as to give her air—she looked up at me.

Even as she was—panting and so small, balled up before me on the concrete—I don't think I'd ever been so frightened by her.

By seeing her there, so close.

Because I think, in the end, those differences aren't so big between us—people and animals. When we communicate from the eyes, it looks the same.

As boys, my brother and I would pull on our waders and set out into the swamp during the long hours after we had finished our homework. We squelched through the mud, laughing at the way our teachers mispronounced words, saying moun-taints and evac-u-nation. The dark, musky water at our waists, and the cottonmouths curled between the cypress knees, their faces furious and their fat bodies unmoving as if petrified—it was all almost enough to entertain us, like it did our Daddy and his Papa before him. We snapped the sharp palmetto leaves at their stems and tossed them into the stand-still bayou, like how we imagined Yankee students might skip rocks on the lakes by their brick-and-ivy prep schools. Eventually, our leaves would fade from sight, though we couldn't tell if it was the current that had taken them from us, or the darkness swelling beneath the branches of the cypress trees.

On our way back home, feeling our way through the trees, hearing that dense chorus of bullfrogs in the dark, we would see them—the Will o' the Wisps. I hear at universities they reconcile those pale, floating lights as phosphorus oxidizing from the dead life of the swamp. If that's all, then it's a bulb of glowing gas that can follow alongside a person, looking like hope, keeping pace. Always ten or twenty yards away, always out of reach. There's a long history of people who have followed their glow, thinking it the porch light of a home on the edge of the city, or the lamp of a neighbor who will lead them out, only to find themselves lost and drifting out where the water is deepest.

Once, as we passed a Wisp, like a pale flower's bloom, flickering at us behind a growth of cattails, my brother turned to me and asked whether someday I'd pick up and leave. Go north, somewhere far from moss-bent trees and the humidity, where there wouldn't be the smell of wet decay that clung each day to our clothes and skin. I didn't know what to say to him, though I know he wouldn't have asked if he didn't feel that same pull. Maybe I was tempted, but we both knew there never was any leaving. There's no following lights.

Since that day, we've grown old and bald, curled like snakes. The underwater mud sucks hard under our heavy boots. And now, even as we've seen the hurricanes grow stronger, watched them topple the cypresses, leaving them broken, floating husks; even after the Gulf rose up, relentless over the seasons like an unebbing tide, paving smooth our swamp and bayou, our old walking trails and our school, the house our father built— we're still here.

Those strange lights we knew, that drifted around us, have all since dissipated. At night our hands reach for landmarks that no longer exist, and I can't even find the place we buried our mother. Though the waves make our lips salty, and the black water laps upon the stilts of our homes, we're here. We're here where the darkness swells until we can't see the horizon.

DISMEMBER ME
Joanna Rafael Goldberg

In my will, I left my remains to be split evenly by all of my ex-boyfriends. They already had me, might as well take me again.

> To Whom It May Concern,
> I hereby bequeath my body to my ex boyfriends, under the following conditions:
> - I'm still sexy
> - I have never given birth
> - I never turned thirty
> If these conditions are not met, please just put the body of the undersigned in a garbage bag and dispose of it in whatever way is most convenient.
>
> Legally yours,
> Jackie Spiegel

Respectful of my last wishes, the men who used to fuck me gathered to collect their inheritance, 1/5 of my life's work. A gift tag on my crooked big toe read "I'm yours. Willingly, Jackie Spiegel." Albeit oxygen-deprived and stiff, I still looked pretty enough. When I was alive, I danced ballet and made sure to stay hydrated. Treating myself like a rare and expensive harp surely helped preserve my good looks.

In death, a marble slab in a windowless room was the stage. Instead of taffeta, I was draped in a paper sheet. Although rigid and expressionless, the shape of my body flat on the marble was familiar to the cartel of men around me. Had I been swaddled in a quilt, they would have thought I was at rest. In the past, they had all seen me perfectly still, mid-REM, or post little death. Did I look any different to them now? That cadaver was me, just a little later, just a little more dead, closer to festering than ever before.

My beneficiaries agreed to divvy up their loot in order of first to most recent boyfriend. One by one they chose parts, taking turns like they were drafting players for a fantasy football league.

The first, my high school sweetheart, took my tongue and slipped it in a small glass tank. Pink but coated in a foamy grey, the tongue tapped on the glass until the man took it out and cupped it with both hands like a child holds a frog he trapped in the woods. He gave my tongue a little kiss before scolding, "Bad tongue. Naughty tongue."

The second tried to take my tits, but the others protested saying he can't take both in one turn. Choosing the right breast, he took the right nipple off the jug and pinned it to his lapel like a pink bachelor's button.

Number three, my boyfriend from my first summer after I turned twenty-one, twirled my long hair into an intricate braid, snipped it off, and sniffed the entire length before knotting it like a tie around his neck. He will never date anyone as pretty as me again.

Fourth in line, who I had once loved most of all, flicked open the Swiss Army knife I gifted him for Valentine's Day and punctured the skin around my lips in a dotted line. He peeled them off my face and popped them into his mouth. Chew chew smack like bubblegum. He blew my skin into a taut, shining bubble six inches in diameter.

The last man I ever had sex with was boyfriend five, number four's childhood friend who started sleeping with me before four had fallen out of love. Five stuck his index finger right into the middle of the swollen flesh balloon that dropped out of four's mouth, poking a hole in the membrane. The bubble deflated, my lips released air like one last birthday wish.

They bonded as they dissected me. They shared anecdotes, impressions of my orgasms and pouty bad moods. As a joke, number five puppeteered my skull, chattering the jaw. Snap snap—he popped my lungs. The twin organs flew out of my open ribs and whizzed around the room in imperfect loop-de-loops, leaving wrinkled sacks on the floor. Boy two crushed the last air pocket out of one lung with the toe of his combat boots like he was stamping out a cigarette butt. He shouldn't have been there—I never loved him, but he didn't know that.

Body part by body part, they dismembered me until the only thing left on the cold marble slab was my heart, alone and bare and black and blue. Oh, how obvious.

EL MANO NEGRA
Mario J. Gonzales

Once there were fires.

Macario started them, at first in the empty lots dotting our town. Several times I caught him feeding kerosene into trash-filled barrels near the hotel that doubled as a wax museum on weekends. The police were always one step behind as was the whole town who suspected Macario but had no proof.

I even found him in my grandparent's shed, dancing among the preserves— chokecherry jams and the hearts of pickled squash nearly falling from their place in the cupboard. At the end of the dance, Macario would take the meatiest preserves and smash them against the brick wall in the alley where the police captain raced his Enfield motorcycle through on Saturday nights.

"Why are you doing this?" I yelled while trying to stop him.

But I knew why. His father's latest stint in the nearby island prison was for Macario a good reason to set fires, break jars and steal things of little value.

I suppose that's why many called Macario a 'born thief.' Though to me, his face wasn't criminal. The hurting curl of his lips, the arched eyebrows dark as crow's feathers and the gentle slope of his brow gave him the washed look of fresh-made innocence.

Innocent or not, Macario did smash the church's collection box for the blind kids of San Jacinto. It was Easter Sunday and palm fronds littered the church steps. The large evening sky looked down on us and everyone who had gone home after services was sitting down to dinner. You could hear their chattering. The sound of bowls and plates being emptied were everywhere. We were passing by the blind's kid's box in front of the church when Macario said, "Let's open this treasure chest," and then threw it against a ten-foot high black and blue cross. Forty-seven pennies flew into the air before shifting winds turned them into bats that fluttered toward the beach and beyond.

Shortly after destroying the box, Macario went blind. This is what happened. We'd gone to the train station to check-out the migrants who jumped on and off on their way to the United States. Some real beauties showed up and we'd try to get their attention. No dice. Macario thought the girls acted like princesses, "Like they shit silver and exhale gold," he'd say.

The train slowed as it neared the station, with the grinding force of its metal brakes throwing thick orange sparks. Several hit Macario's face. He shrieked, an awful stabbing sound, saying, though I barely understood, "Everything's floating in white light." He tried rubbing vision back into his eyeballs and when he couldn't, Macario pulled at his hair, took out his knife and threatened to tear deep into every shadow, turn each piles of air into piles of ash. I grabbed a nearby brick in case he lashed into me. But the buzz-saw cut of his voice fizzled to a low mumble and he scowled like a young thug glimpsing for a moment their cruel solitude.

On our way home clouds boomed, signaling a monsoon rain that dropped a few meager drops before retreating over the mountains, "The rains are falling in the Huesca Valley. The llano must be green there and the barrancas loaded with wildflowers." I said and then regretted every word, feeling embarrassed at how fruity I sounded. None of it mattered since Macario's mind was elsewhere, ignoring me, so I said without thinking, "You know, your blindness is divine justice, Macario, God's punishment for breaking the coin box."

Quicksilver light blew in and out of his eyes and then came a rage. An awful one, bodied with a crooked spine and the scabbiest of rat bones.

"Fuck the blind kids. Everyone takes a hit. Just like everybody gives one. It's got nothing to do with God. It's all crazy, anyway. Even normal things are crazy stuff in disguise. Like did you know that my mom's new husband was already married to a Tres Lagunas woman? Yeah, he told her after the wedding, wouldn't shut up about it, proud of having two women, I guess. That's how it is, Ludo. Makes no sense, none."

I said nothing and walked ahead of Macario who held onto my belt and made small rings of dust twirl like yellow devils at his feet.

After a short while, Macario's eyes lolled side-to-side as if he were having a seizure. The wind blew a wicked gust of the sun's fire onto our backs. I'd stopped to look up the road at some men fixing a flat tire. Oil and sweat poured from their foreheads. Engine sounds came out of their mouths and their teeth were as sharp and uneven as broken glass. Afraid, I turned to Macario. His mini-seizure had ended, all the stiff muscles masking his face let go. With his pain and tension eased, Macario pushed back his shoulders like a bird readying itself for flight and began talking about his old man,

"My father was happiest when he could pick locks, lift wallets, plunder stores. He especially loved the trick action of a switchblade. He called it his dancing partner."

Macario then showed me the spot on his knee where his father had jabbed a knifepoint years ago. I said the scar was shaped like a clown's smile. Macario thought it was more like a baboon's skull.

"And Ludo," he said, drawing me so close I felt the thump of his heartbeat crash into mine, "Few know, but my father was sick, ulcers on his chest, bleeding ones. But get this, the ulcers gave him visions and he'd see El Mano Negra rising like the dead from the sea."

Macario suddenly changed topics, saying innocently enough,

"Hey Ludo, describe the trees, the dirt lots filled with dead cars. Describe the statue of a fat baby riding a sea turtle in the center of the park."

"Don't be ass. You know what they look like. They haven't changed since yesterday," I said, not knowing why I spoke like a muddy creature to Macario, my best and only friend.

I then paused and thought about the childhood we'd shared: throwing white slimy stones at pirated ships from the banks of Cienfuego cove. Or sleeping as one in tattered hammocks thin as spider webs, our bellies limp from hunger. Dreaming about calabash flower soup and waking with a jicaro taste in our mouths.

Macario also stopped and stood before me: eyes useless, shirt off, back sloped as if he were expecting a hit. It came from the muddy creature as I pushed Macario. He fell, hitting the ground hard.

When he did, time splintered, the moment cracking in two. Then I remembered a great slowing. I was sure of this as I could hear the old men waiting for a barber's shave clear dust from their throats and picture the ash from the trash pit fires fall like little bits of hell swarming. It was like a beam of light shining through darkness allowing me to clearly see Macario as he was now and would be forever. In that place I saw the sweat living on Macario's chest roll downward. I saw its electric path flow to his stomach where it disappeared at the border separating his tanned waist and shorts. And when he opened his mouth to speak, I saw heat blossom full upon his lips and could sense the soft wet reaches of his tongue, lifting, curling, arching. It was a kiss. Made from the waters of some inconsolable dream.

When the world started-up again, Macario had his finger in my face, shouting awful things about my family. How my uncle Ribero, lost at sea, was queer; how my grandmother's dread of being photographed and my grandfather's fallen arches were proof they lived in constant fear. He grabbed the shirt slung over his shoulder and tried to strangle me. He was strong as a stone cutter's grip, but my knee found his balls and I gave him a good one.

"Go the fuck home, you thief," I yelled. Macario staggered, with nowhere to go, past the sterile fig trees we use to climb as boys and the thorny bits of grass our senile mayor dares to call a park.

Feeling odd, with only time to lose, I held sand dollars to my eyes trying to figure out what the blind see. The brittle shells felt ancient and something emerged from the one pushed against my right eye. Removing the dollar, I saw a tiny worm poking its body from a hole. Meanwhile, Macario had snuck behind and punched me hard right center on my back.

"What the hell? I thought you were blind."

"Only in one eye. Come on, it's getting late. Let's go to the beach."

On the beach, ocean turtles would crawl on their bellies to lay eggs. Macario got it in his head that his father would escape prison by dressing as a turtle and swim unrecognized among them. We spent the night, a moonless one, watching the turtles enter and leave the beach after doing their business. I fell asleep. When I woke in the morning Macario was covered in seaweed, eating turtle eggs. They made him retch and I said with a voice scratched and pitted, "It serves you right."

Tired from lack of sleep, Macario passed out on the shore. The tide licked at his toes as I watched over him, brushing away the speckled sand crabs. While he slept, I built a castle wall from cracked and worn shells littering the beach to protect us from the hurly-burly cries of inmates imprisoned across the sea. Talking from the confined space of his firelit visions, Macario raved about El Mano Negra using words only the condemned could understand.

After his long sleep, Macario woke-up and we watched the tides shrink and grow. I asked him about the fires, if they'd ever stop. He looked at the ground, searched for a firmness that wasn't there and said, "Everything burns eventually, Ludo. Didn't your grandparents ever teach you that?"

■ ■ ■

"At first sign of more trouble we'll jump into the ocean, hand in hand. If it rains, we'll open our umbrellas and dare lightning to strike us twice."

I said this to Macario the next time we met. One of his eyes was bandaged and so we walked carefully through a weedy field. Half of it was stubble while the other half was overgrown and golden, deep with insects. Whenever the wind changed directions small locusts popped into the air. One caught in the tangled strands of Macario's long dirty hair. Without moving his head, he reached for the grasshopper, crushing it in his palm.

"Tough guy," I said. He shrugged and with the back of his hand felt for a mustache he'd been trying to grow for months but his face was always too young, too soft.

In the evening, we saw the lighthouse light was off and the bats had gone, resting in their caves. Their bellies are full we both said at the same time. We pinched each other's arm and noticed how sad the sea was. No waves and it looked like an endless cemetery with the white and black seabirds listlessly gliding just above the water. We had nowhere to go and all day to get there. Everyone else: the shellfish poachers, the head-scarfed practitioners of Santeria and the hollowed-out junkies who peddled their bodies for a taste of morphine had gone home. All was quiet, and the silence was brutal. We camped at a rock called Whale Maiden. I sat on the tail and Macario lay like a murder victim across the hump.

In a voice burned green, lazy with sun and salt, Macario said, "I'm bored. Tell me a story, Ludo, make it a good one."

"We're the last humans in the world," I began.

"The earth is doomed. Earthquakes, floods and fires are near. But we don't care and so as we wait for the ruin to begin, we learn to hover like colorful kites in the sky. We pass the time climbing snow-capped mountains and racing miniature peacocks on motorbikes through fern and redwood forests. When we get hungry you roast fish and pig: cabrillo and acamaya and give me the fattest portions of roasted pork ever seen. We eat till our eyes grow tight and small. Then we smoke cigarillos. Black-tongued river monkeys from the far side of the mountains come to gamble with us. They offer gifts: elephant whistles and cherry bark candies. In return, we teach them to read the flights of birds for signs of the apocalypse."

More silence came and then it died, killed by sirens. We weren't the last people on earth anymore. There were others and they meant to take Macario away.

EL MANO NEGRA CAUGHT!!!

That was the newspaper headline announcing Macario's capture.

An epidemic of rats at the police station led to the cops being out full force and there was Macario, kerosene in hand, about to douse the police captain's beloved motorcycle. 'We've got you,' they said with faces screaming like men trapped inside carnival mirrors. Macario sneered, filled his breath with the poisons corroding his soul and lunged at their throats. They attacked. Blinding him once more by pouring salt directly into his eyes and then throwing him in a dirty cell where he gorged on rats and nothing else. After a week, Macario was released on the condition he leave town and never return.

Once free, Macario said, "There's not a prison alive that can hold me. Give me the keys to the cell, I'll burn them. The houses, the barns, the fisherman's boats, I'll burn it all."

That same night the lighthouse light blinked meaning someone had escaped. Prison boats made their way to land. Macario believed it was his father. Later we heard the escapee had drowned. Eaten by sharks was what the pimple-nosed barber told us after returning from shaving the heads of one hundred prisoners.

"Who was he?" we asked.

"Who knows and who the hell cares," he said. "It's a well-known fact that the world does better without lice-infested men."

Later that week, I went to my cousin Miguel's wedding in Primavera. I drank too much and spent most of the night at the top of the stairs in the dance hall. My Tia Marci came to me, felt my forehead and asked why I was so cold.

"I'm not cold," I said, knowing full well that while everything else moved with fever, I stayed frozen like a frightened rabbit.

"You can't fool me. I gave you the touch. You're cold and in this heat, it's no wonder you don't fall dead right here. Let me see something else," she said and then pinched the back of neck until there was popping sound that echoed against the wall.

"Cold. You've been visited by El Mano Negra. I'm never wrong about these things. Never. I have something for you." She went downstairs and returned with two tacos stuffed with meat.

"Here, eat."

"What's in it," I asked

"Axolotl mixed with some burrowing owl," she replied. "Eat it all. Don't even think about leaving a crumb for the saints. Those nags can find their own food."

I ate both tacos and quickly passed out.

My Tia's words rolled inside me restlessly, picking at my thoughts, so the next time I saw Macario I asked, "Do you believe in El Mano Negra? That it is what people say?"

He was drinking mulberry wine, the worst of all wines. And after hearing my question, the blackened copper in his eyes flashed and he drunkenly said to get my head straight. "Ludo, soon I'll be in Villahermosa with my mother and bastard stepfather. He has a bar there. I'll spend my time selling shrimp cocktails to fat tourists with fatter wallets. El Mano Negra? Give me a fucking break."

I stretched my bones like a cat climbing out of a box and considered selling everything I had and moving to Villahermosa. For a minute or two I saw this dream and then looked at the reality of the land. The ground is harder than a pick-axe and so nothing grows. The air boils in the summer and the fish stink of oil and gas. My pockets are always empty and it's no wonder that the people here fear their dead. Many choosing to lock them away in caves and under limestone barrancas outside of town.

This was my home, where I belonged, I concluded:

"Right, no big deal. Let's go," I said. A diesel truck almost hit us as I led Macario across a road. The driver stared us down. Macario returned the stare, his blind eyes not moving until the driver blasted his horn.

That night I lay in bed, thinking about how Macario would soon join his stepfather and mother somewhere far away. Outside my window, a blue iguana sat on the lowest bough of a dried-up rosewood tree while I sulked and repeatedly said, "We'll walk into the ocean some other time. When we're old men. When our backs are hollowed, our eyes opened."

Soon after, I visited my Tia Marci at her house. She was working: reading the lives of people through their hands. When I entered the room, my Tia rose from her seat and with a panic in her voice said,

"Dios mio, my body hurts with the sight of you. You're even colder. What a shame the angels would rather carouse with strangers than help my people. Well, no one ever got rich in a confessional. Give me your hands."

I gave her my hands which she rubbed thoroughly with talcum powder. She then took out a large aspirin, cut it in two and offered me one half while she swallowed the other. "I've had a bitch of a headache all day," she said after blowing her nose and sending away a pockmarked child who came in search of his father. "That boy," Tia Marci said, pointing to the fatherless kid walking out the door, "will never stop looking until one day he will become rough. His eyes will fail. His scent will turn to sulphur. Not even El Mano Negra would dare cast a shadow past his early grave."

"El Mano Negra?" I answered while the fan overhead spun unevenly. I worried that time was splintering again since outside the evening's blue light sang a cowardly song. It covered everything in a foul wind and an ash that floated like a plague in the air. Everyone in town felt it too, causing upheaval. Windows were shuttered, doors locked and the sound of a thousand rosary novenas ate deep into my heart. Even Tia Marci was forced to snuff out her candles and light new ones in their place, saying as she did,

"You know, El Mano Negra was once promised to the sun. But he fell to earth one day disguised as rain. And people crazy with love and fear, dressed him in paper clothing and danced around him until his soul caught fire. He then became an orphan, a black coral snake, the moonless sea, the enemy of time and possessor of the dawn." Tia Marci then studied my face for a while. In an almost-whisper she finally told me what I already knew, "Your heat will return but your sleep will always run cold."

She then gave me a black coral amulet saying as I left, "Steal the words of Santerians and make an offering to the sea where El Mano Negra dies and is reborn." I went home, and tired of time playing its tricks, I snuck into my grandfather's room and took a prized watch from his dresser. Just before dawn I walked to the beach, dug a hole well deep and buried the watch. Then I filled my mouth with sea water, twisted its bitter taste through my tongue and spat out the residue on the watch's grave. Thinking that I could steady the burning world by removing its most potent fires. Finally, I prayed, begging El Mano Negra to lift sight back into his Macario's eyes. So that he could see the world as I did.

Then I waited for daylight and for Macario who agreed to one last meeting on the red-clay rooftop of the hotel that doubles as a wax museum on weekends.

But everything continued to burn just as Macario predicted. Caught in the flames were the late spring flowers on the hillside that withered and the little fish in the shallows of the sea that disappeared. I remember watching the fires from a distance, standing with Macario on the rooftop overlooking the sea. "Let's jump, Ludo," he shouted. I hesitated, thinking we'd break our necks. But jumped anyway, landing softly on the beach. The muddy creature returned and animating my voice, spoke to Macario, "You're a thief, an arsonist. If you keep it up, you'll end up in prison just like your dad."

Macario laughed, "Don't say nothing, Ludo. Ever since we've been kids, I've gotten into trouble and then you warn me about this or that. I break and burn stuff, steal things that need to be stolen. I don't do nothing else. Don't want to."

"But you'll be locked up," I said.

"You never can see that we're all in jail, all of us prisoners of something. Look at the houses, at their bars and fences. What does that say?"

"They're houses, Macario, people just wanting safety."

"Safety? What makes them safe? You tell me. People are afraid, that's all they are. Everyone hiding from their shadow. First, they get rid of my dad acting like this keeps them safe. But it never does. Cause what people really know, all they know is fear. Okay, they'll get rid of me, later it'll be another. You'll see, Ludo. You'll see someday. Carry me to the rocks where the tide pools collect."

Armies of sand fleas crawled under our skin as I carried Macario on my back from where he whispered in my ear, "Ludo, someday you'll need to break every goddamn jar in your grandparent's lousy shed."

On that day, sand flew on my wet lips and Macario tore my shirt, the one that read, 'Life is love.' He then held me. He held me closer than the wind before letting go. I fell, hitting the shore. It was there I saw dozens of hungry ravens soar overhead and heard children baying like wolves at my sadness. But I didn't care. "The doomed earth is ours," I shouted long after Macario's mother and stepfather had come and taken him away.

At dawn, river monkeys appeared, singing songs about the water and begging for safe passage through my sprawling sorrow. I bowed yes and so did they. Our shadows mixing in front of great roasting fires. The air smelled of pork drippings and fish oils and orange embers singed the banners of a vacant heaven. Still it was not enough. Macario had disappeared. It was then I knew that no amount of Tia Marci's divinations would save us from the black-handed one; the one that tricks and splinters time; the one whose fires burn wild, as if they were not even fires at all but only some kind of spell that comes and stays and never leaves.

That was long ago. But ever since on those nights I can't sleep, I'll go to the beach and watch one hundred fugitive men rise from the ocean and walk onto the shore. Unlike fire they seem solid, with their shaved heads wet from a moonless sea and their mournful prisoner movements scorched from years behind bars. And while they go slowly, moving as if they're entering a dream, I've wondered, and always will, if El Mano Negra walks among them.

PIECES
Pete Hsu

Penny Leong is eight-years-old and home by herself. At the kitchen table, she is playing at organizing a large extended family of toys. She arranges them with the strong toys along a perimeter surrounding the gentler ones. As she plays, a loud knock from the front door startles her. Penny freezes. She stops in mid-motion. She holds her breath and stretches out her hands across the table hovering over the toys like a protective mother blanketing her children from harm. Just out of her reach is a Yellow Power Ranger action figure. The Yellow Ranger stands still. It is stationed on the furthest edge of the table, the strongest of Penny's toys. The Ranger's form is feminine like a Barbie doll. It is dressed in a comic book superhero costume. It wears a mask. It holds a laser rifle. It has a missing leg. It starts to teeter.

Penny shushes the Ranger, "Stay still."

But it falls. Penny gasps. Then another knock at the door.

Another gasp. She stumbles to her feet and then is still again. She places both hands over her mouth. The knocking stops. She takes a deep breath and decides that, despite being scared, she should investigate. She exhales and makes her way to the front door. She steps only on the floorboards that don't squeak. At the door, she peers through the scratched and foggy peephole. The features of the person on the other side are blurred, but Penny can tell who it is by his bulk and his slouch. It's Gerald. Gerald is her mother's ex-husband. Gerald is Penny's ex-stepfather.

"Lucky," he says, his voice booming, "I know you're there. I can see you through the peephole."

She thinks that he probably can't see her through the peephole. She doesn't know this for certain. She ducks down. She puts her hands on the doorknob, not yet turning it. Gerald knocks again.

"Come on, girl. It's baba. Open up."

"You're not my baba."

"Oh come on," Gerald laughs, holding up a large rectangular case, "Look here. I got something. I promise, you're gonna like it."

Penny peers through the scope of the peephole. One eye closed. One eye open. She focuses between the scratchy lenses to find a small clear window. She looks at the case. It's long and black with chrome trim. On the front is a small brass plate bolted onto the black plastic. The plate has a lightning bolt on it. It looks like the Power Rangers logo. Penny knows Gerald used to be some kind of ranger. He could have been a Power Ranger. But that's stupid. But still, maybe.

She turns the knob slightly. Gerald pushes through as soon as there's give in the door. He does this with authority, but not with violence. Penny is moved aside. Gerald walks in. As he passes, he pats her on the head. He says, "There we are, how's my Lucky Penny, huh?"

Her hair is mangled. It is tied into two uneven pigtails. Gerald grabs one pigtail and tugs on it. Penny relaxes a little bit, remembering how kind he could be. He puts down the long, rectangular case and squats next to her. He looks at her. He opens his arms. She hugs him. His shirt smells like dirt and cigarettes. His skin smells like beer.

Gerald lets Penny go and heads into the kitchen. He picks up a bowl of cereal. It is one of three that Penny has rationed for the day. He scoops two spoonfuls into his mouth. It crunches as he chews. Still holding the bowl, he rummages through the refrigerator. He complains that there isn't anything decent to drink, and then returns with a mostly empty two-liter bottle of store brand cola and a mostly full bottle of Tom Araby's London Dry Gin. The gin is kept in the freezer. It has frost on its label.

Gerald sits down at the dining table. He pushes aside Penny's toys. He puts the bottles and a plastic tumbler down next to the Yellow Ranger. Gerald picks the Ranger up, running his thumb over the female anatomy of the plastic figure. A bolt of protectiveness jolts Penny. She wants to rescue the toy. She wants to snatch the figure out of Gerald's hand. She doesn't do it. She is scared to provoke him. He looks up from the toy. He looks at Penny. He smiles, putting the figure down, carefully bending it at its one remaining knee, adjusting it so that it balances on its one remaining foot. He then fixes himself a gin and coke. He takes a sip.

"Bleh, tastes like shit," he says with enthusiasm, before drinking the rest and then pouring himself another.

"Mama'll be back soon," says Penny, even though she doesn't know when her mother will return.

"No, she won't," he says, his head bobbing in small circles. "Your mama's working. Right? Your mother, the worker bee. And she's working today. And tonight. All night. Right?"

Gerald grins and raises his eyebrows.

"No," Penny says, "She'll be back very, very soon."

"Quit. Ain't no secrets between us," he says. "Or maybe she's got secrets from you. But Baba Gerald knows all."

Penny purses her lips, angry that she doesn't know how to respond to this, and afraid that it's true.

"Besides," Gerald continues. "I am not here for your mom. I am here for you."

He taps his forefinger on the table as he says this last part. I. Tap. Am. Tap. Here. Tap. For you. Tap. Tap. Tap. As he does this, Penny watches her toys jostle on the table with each tap. They bounce, jarred as if caught in a tiny earthquake. At the last tap, the Yellow Ranger falls over. Penny reaches out and grabs it. As she clutches the toy, Gerald reaches out and grabs Penny's hand.

"You still playing with dolls?" he asks, holding her hand. She can feel the Yellow Ranger's pointy foot dig into her palm. Gerald shakes his head as if to clear his eyesight and then nods towards the case. "I think it's time to grow up. Put aside childish things."

Gerald takes another moment to focus and then gets up to retrieve the case. He yanks it off the ground, flinging it through the air and then uses it to swipe everything off the table. The bottles, his cup, and all of Penny's toys. Everything lands on to the kitchen floor with a clatter. Gerald laughs and fumbles with the combinations on the case latches. He turns the wheels over and over. Penny is tentative, but she leans forward. She's still holding the toy in one hand, but places the other on Gerald's shoulder. He undoes that last latch. He throws up the case. He shouts, "Voila!"

Penny crowds in. She's smushed into Gerald's side. She drops the action figure and places both hands on the edge of the case. Her eyes are open wide and her jaw slackens. Inside the case, surrounded by fitted green velvet is a long, black rifle.

Penny nods and looks at Gerald. She says, "Wow."

"Yeah," says Gerald. "You like it. Course you do."

"Mama won't like it."

"Well good thing she ain't here then," he says.

Penny takes a small step backwards, away from the rifle. "Where did you get this?"

"Bought it."

Penny knows that this shouldn't be true. She knows Gerald isn't allowed to do certain things, like vote or work in a casino or re-enlist, or buy a gun.

He takes the rifle out. He now seems much more sober. His movements seem controlled and deliberate. He holds the rifle with his right hand, his palm on the grip, his forefinger resting on the outer rim of the trigger guard. Penny stares at the rifle. She takes in its insistent simplicity. It is different from her toy guns that are ornamented with endless buttons and switches, lights and speakers, plugs and attachments. Gerald's rifle is smooth and clean and singular in purpose.

He holds it out to her. "Go on, girl. Take it. It's fine. It ain't loaded."

She takes the rifle with both hands. From stock to barrel, it is just a tad shorter than she is. She seems to have a general sense of how to carry the rifle. She holds it with great balance, as if it is an extension of her arm. Gerald nudges her. She pulls the rifle up, resting the stock in the crook of her shoulder. Gerald starts to help her position it, but then stops, saying, "You done this before, Lucky?"

The rifle is light in her arms, far lighter than she would ever have imagined a real gun would weigh. She stares down the sight, closing one eye.

"Both eyes open," says Gerald. He places a hand on her shoulder. "You need to see everything."

She opens both eyes and adjusts her vision. She lines up the rear sight to the front. She aims at the broken toaster across the room. Pow. She aims at the stack of bills on the countertop. Pow. She aims across the living room at the television. Pow. She aims at her torn-up backpack. Pow. Her mother's high-heeled cowboy boots. Pow. The upright fan. Pow. The dusty faux sunflowers. Pow. The cracked frame with the old picture of Gerald and her mother standing on the steps of some fancy brick building, Gerald thin with crew-cut hair and a heather gray *Army of One* T-shirt, Penny's mom young and clear-eyed and ready to make a difference in the world, the two of them not yet aware that their love will sour, and that their lives will soon spiral out of control. Penny pulls the trigger. It's soft and doesn't click. But in her head, Pow. Pow. Pow.

Penny stops and looks at Gerald.

He says, "Better days, right, Lucky?"

He walks across the room and takes the picture off the wall. He opens the back of the frame. He takes the photograph out. He looks at it for what seems like a long time before easing it into his jacket pocket. He finishes the rest of his drink and claps his hands together. "Get your coat. Let's go shoot."

■ ■ ■

Gerald drives her out a long way. They go through the city and up into the mountains. They pass at least one shooting range on the way. Penny can see it from the freeway. She asks why they don't go there, but Gerald brushes it off as "regulations." Penny thinks this is related the Gerald's probation. She is concerned that they might get in trouble. She worries about being caught by the police or by her mother. She worries about Gerald himself.

They get into the winding switchbacks of the mountains. Gerald rolls down the windows. The air is cold and bites at the insides of Penny's nose. She takes a breath as big as she can. She exhales unevenly. She's afraid. She doesn't like this feeling of being afraid. It's confusing. She's not sure what she's afraid of. She is afraid of Gerald. But she's also glad to be with him. She's afraid of her mother. She's afraid that her mother will be angry with her when she finds out she went with Gerald. She's also afraid her mother will be sad and that Penny will feel like that is her fault, that the sadness is her fault. She closes her eyes. The sadness seeps into her. She doesn't resist. Her head feels heavy. She lays her head down in Gerald's lap. As she starts to fall asleep, she says in a voice that is not audible in the noisy cab of the truck, "Night night, Baba."

■ ■ ■

"Wakey wakey," says Gerald when they arrive at their destination. "We're here."

Penny is already half-awake when she hears his voice. She pops up and flings open the door to Gerald's pickup truck. They're parked in a dirt clearing. There aren't any other cars. There are tall pine trees and large boulders in the distance. Closer is a fallen tree trunk. Gerald is opening the gun case and taking out the rifle. He removes the bolt from the rifle and looks down the bore and then through the open sights and then through the bore and then the sights again. He makes adjustments in between views. He does this several times and then reinstalls the bolt and places the rifle back in the open case. He then begins filling the cartridge with rounds of .243. Gerald explains this caliber is light enough for a child to handle, but strong enough to bring down a deer with a single shot. An important feature, he insists, so that the wounded animal doesn't run off into the woods to bleed out over the course of hours, or worse, to be maimed but not killed, becoming some kind of aberration, ostracized, starving and alone.

"Decisive," he says, a brightness in his voice. "Like flipping a switch. No questions. No take backs. No negotiations. No hesitations, consultations or explanations. Just wham, bam, thank you ma'am."

Gerald seems mostly sober now, as if the drive and the fresh air rejuvenated him. But he's brought the bottle of Araby's. It protrudes from Gerald's back pocket. Gerald inserts the cartridge and shoulders the rifle. He takes a plastic garbage bag full of recyclables. Penny recognizes the bag from the apartment.

Gerald walks into the distance. He walks towards the fallen pine tree. There he arranges the cans and bottles along the top of it. He puts up five targets, one for each round in the magazine. He drops the bag with the remaining targets. He walks back to Penny. There's a bit of a spring to his step.

Penny remembers Gerald arguing with her mother about guns. There had been a shooting three cities over. Gerald had been drunk and in tears watching the television reports of children being gunned down in a cafeteria. He'd said, "Those poor bastards hadn't had a chance." Gerald wanted to buy a gun in case anything like that happened around them. Her mother said it wasn't a good idea. Gerald said they need protection. He said the world is gone to shit. Her mother called him a drunk and an idiot. Gerald warned her to not antagonize him. She said she wasn't. Gerald said she was, she always was.

Penny had then changed television channel. She didn't want to see any more about the shooting. Gerald yelled at her for changing the television channel because isn't it obvious that he was still watching that. She changed it back. He kicked a hole in the wall. Her mother screamed at Gerald to leave Penny alone. Gerald knocked her mother down and kicked her. Penny hid in her room, in the dark, in the corner of her closet. She thought about the kids who'd been shot.

■ ■ ■

"Okay, this is twenty-five yards," says Gerald, marking the ground with the heel of his shoe. "Follow me."

She follows him to the next marker. "This is fifteen."

Then to the next. "This is ten."

With that, Gerald pivots on his heel, pulling the rifle up to his shoulder as he does. He lands on both feet, turning to face the targets. He fires in one fluid motion. The rifle cracks with a loud pop. Penny covers her ears and closes her eyes. When she opens them, she sees Gerald. He is frowning.

"Shit," he says. "Missed."

He takes the rifle up again. He steadies himself. He takes his time to line up this next shot. Penny can hear him breathing. He inhales a gulp of air. He exhales. He pulls the trigger. He misses again.

"Holy fuck," he says, as if surprised. "Hold on. One more."

He tries again. He misses again. He props the rifle against his leg and takes the bottle of Araby's from his pants pocket. He uncorks it and takes a steady sip. He wipes his mouth with his sleeve. As he puts the bottle back, he picks up the rifle and hands it to Penny.

"Whattaya say, Lucky? Give it a shot?"

Penny takes the rifle. She lowers it, barrel pointing to the ground. She places her right hand on the small metal ball of the bolt, lifts it and pulls a round into the chamber. She brings the rifle back up, up to the crook of her shoulder, like she did at the apartment. She does this with quiet seriousness. Gerald doesn't need to warn her not to point that thing at him or to keep her finger off the trigger until she's ready to shoot. It's as if she knows these things already. He helps her with her stance. With a couple of taps on her feet, she balances her weight and levels the rifle steady, its 22-inch barrel parallel with the Earth. He stands behind her. He tells her to brace herself against him. She leans on his hip. He says, "Try to stay loose. This shit gonna kick."

Penny fixes her eyes on the fallen trunk. She thinks about which target she wants to shoot. Roving from a soda can to a wine bottle to an unopened can of soup or enchilada sauce. She imagines the cans and bottles as villains. She imagines them lurking in the distance, advancing on her. She imagines them close, very close, at her front door. There you are. She looks into the eyes of her adversary. She imagines herself as the Yellow Ranger. The strongest. She takes in an even breath and pulls the trigger. There's a flash in her retina, a searing pain in her shoulder. A tin can explodes.

"Holy shit!" exclaims Gerald. "Oh my God, Lucky, you did it! Try again!"

Penny doesn't respond to Gerald's praise. She cocks the rifle and braces herself against his leg again. She aims and fires. The wine bottle shatters. Gerald taps her shoulder and motions for the rifle. She gives it to Gerald. He reloads the cartridge. He does this quickly. He hands the rifle back to her.

"Okay, baby girl. Back up to the fifteen."

She backs up. He follows but stands a bit away.

"Now, you don't need me. Go on. Do it."

She does. She fires. Her small frame adapts quickly and absorbs the kick without much fanfare. Over on the log, the soda can is knocked off. She continues: a blue water bottle, a row of three empty cans of light beer. Bam. Bam. Bam. Gerald applauds after each. When they're all knocked off, he hurries back to the log and puts more targets up. She hits them all. He reloads the rifle and again sets up more targets. He calls out each, far left, middle, near left, far right, last one. She hits each, on demand, as called. They move back to the twenty-five-yard mark. He calls out the targets again. She hits them all again.

Gerald is beside himself. "A natural, baby! You are a bona fides natural! Goddammit I gotta take your ass to the county fair."

He continues to drink from the bottle of Araby's. It still looks halfway full. He laughs and hugs Penny. She doesn't hug him back. She can feel the ache in her shoulder and the fatigue in her arms and her legs. But she doesn't want to stop.

Gerald loses his balance. He falls to the ground. He pulls Penny down next to him. He says, "Why you," and tickles her. She's not ticklish. He stops. They lie on their sides, facing each other. She looks at Gerald. His hair is in his eyes. He is smiling and looking back at her, staring really.

"You're beautiful, Lucky. You know that?" he says.

She looks away, neither glad nor embarrassed.

"For real. You are. Jesus, I wish I could see you grown up."

"I'll be grown up soon," she says.

"Yeah, but if your mama has her way, I won't be around to see it," he says.

Penny looks at him, studying his face. His smile fades and his eyes drop.

"Why?" she asks, but she already knows why.

"I'm sorry, baby," he says, "But she's right. I'm no good for you. I haven't been good. I haven't been around, when you all needed me. You did need me. You needed somebody to look after you. Keep you safe."

Penny doesn't respond. She thinks about being safe. She's surprised at how odd that word lands on her mind. Like a leaf from a strange tree from a very far-away place.

Penny looks at the rifle. It's propped up next to them, against the fallen trunk. Gerald reaches over and brushes the back of his hand against Penny's cheek. Penny flinches just a little bit. Gerald puts his hand at the back of her neck. She pulls away, scrambling to get her footing.

"Hey, Whoa, Lucky," says Gerald, sitting up fast, holding his hands out. "Whoa. What's happening, kid? I ain't gonna hurt you. I wouldn't ever hurt you."

Penny backs up.

"Come on, Lucky. Don't be mad at me."

"I'm not mad," she says. She turns and looks at the rifle again. Gerald watches her. She wonders if she can reach it before he can stop her.

"What are you thinking, Lucky? What's in that head of yours?"

"Nothing," she says.

"Nothing?"

"Nothing."

"Okay, now come on," says Gerald, his hands still up and open. "You wanna be the hunter now, little miss Earn'st Hemingway? You wanna hunt? Waddaya say I take you on safari?"

The idea attracts Penny's attention. Gerald gets on to his feet and tucks the bottle away. He picks up the rifle and holds it out to her. She takes it. He says, "I didn't mean nothing," and adjusts the rifle strap on Penny's shoulder. She nods. They go forward into the woods.

■ ■ ■

Every few minutes Gerald stops and makes a show of tracking something. He picks up a broken twig or sniffs at brush or checks out what might be a paw print in the mud. Each time he finds a clue, he takes a slow and focused sip from the bottle and, with dramatic seriousness, waves his hand at Penny and points forward, deeper into the trees.

Some short time later, Gerald and Penny come into a grassy clearing in between a stretch of brush and an array of big southern live oak trees. Gerald drops onto the ground, flat on his back. He stares up into the atmosphere. It's close to dusk. The sun is still lighting up the sky in a full blue, but the shadows are long. The temperature is starting to drop. Penny lays down next to Gerald. She can smell the sour sweat on him along with the oddly clean smell of the gin. He puts an arm over her and says, "Jesus, Lucky. I think I'm drunk." Penny lets the weight of his arm settle. It's heavy. It crushes her a little bit. But she doesn't mind it.

As she lies beside him, Penny sees something. It's in the distance. It's a small stout figure. She pulls away from the crook of Gerald's elbow. She sits up cross-legged. She takes the rifle off her shoulder. Gerald turns to look in the direction Penny is looking. "What is it, Lucky?"

She points to the brush, to a large oak standing out in front of it. The tree's trunk looks as thick as Gerald's pickup. Seven large branches reach out and up from the base. A shadow the size of a large dog moves slowly in front of the tree.

"Oh dang," says Gerald. "A bear cub? What the hell's she doing out here?"

Penny lifts the rifle to her shoulder. She bows her back to hunch over the sights. She aims at the baby bear. Gerald grabs her leg.

"Lucky, wait. Wait."

Penny steadies herself. She hears Gerald but doesn't lower the rifle. She sees the cub's head. She lines up the front sight with the rear, aiming at the animal's forehead. She inhales and rubs the trigger guard with the pad of her forefinger.

Gerald pats her on the leg. "Lucky, wait."

She exhales, keeping the rifle steady.

Still on his back, Gerald eases himself up onto one elbow. "Now look. You cannot shoot that cub."

"Why?" asks Penny.

"Because it's wrong, baby girl. That cub's just a kid, like you."

Penny thinks for a second. "But that doesn't matter. That cub's a bear. Bears are strong and mean. They kill people. We need to stop them."

"Well, now. Maybe. But there's something else."

Penny takes one eye off the sights and looks to Gerald.

He continues, "That cub, she's supposed to stay there by that tree, close. The tree's supposed to be her sitter."

"Bear cubs have babysitters?" asks Penny.

"Well, yes they do. Their mothers leave them by these trees," Gerald's voice drops. "But I'm telling you, you fire that gun, that mother bear's gonna be on us quick. Maybe we'll have five minutes. But maybe we won't have even one. And an angry mother bear, shit, girl, you can pump that Remington empty into her, and she'd still tear us both to pieces."

"I'm not afraid," she says, pulling the bolt and bringing a new round into the chamber.

"It's not about being afraid, Lucky."

"It is," she says.

Gerald scoots a little further back. He places one hand softly on the top of the rifle, over the barrel, covering the rear sight. He says, "You gotta trust me on this, kid. A mother bear's not fucking around when it comes to her babies."

Penny stares through Gerald's hand. She can see a line from the rifle's sights across the field and into the cub. The line is clear, as if drawn with a ruler across a long sheet of vellum. She thinks about the mother bear. She imagines it. It is covered in bristled fur and thick sinewy muscle. Penny imagines it standing tall on its hind legs. It towers over Penny and over Gerald too. It towers over the trees, over the mountains, over the Earth itself. Penny imagines it snarling, its teeth long and sharp with foamy spit dripping off. She imagines it growling. The growling like a language. It is a language that only a few know. The language of the strong directed at the weak. The language that burrows into the skulls of the vulnerable, echoing against the shone alabaster walls of dark closets and tightly shut eyes. Penny moves her forefinger from the guard onto the trigger.

"Hey, hey," says Gerald, his hand still laid on top of the rifle. "Come on, girl."

She blinks. Tears welled in her eyes drop onto her cheeks.

"No," she says.

"Lucky," he says. "Whatever you're thinking."

Penny squeezes the trigger. The rifle fires. Gerald screams. He pulls his hand off the barrel. In the distance the bear cub falls. Penny rises to her feet. She reloads the rifle. From the brush, a frantic rustling.

POETRY

THE LISTENING
James Hoch

Snow again, I can't hear it falling
in birches, yard, garden beds, heady
tufts and root down of winter carrots,
though I stare out there, as if
listening to the making. The way,
a kid, I'd rise in the middle of night
looking for my father, who was
as present as absence, the house
the usual dark I'd sleep walk through.
Eventually someone would find me
sitting on the living room floor,
W-sitting, snow on television, or
looking canvas-blank out a window,
eyes open but not seeing. *Snowman*,
they'd call, nudge me back from sleep,
silence cracking like a crocus—
The reveal, all that breaking, a kiss.
I don't know if I loved anything more.
When my father died, a backhoe broke
the sky open, which filled with crows,
and a dusting coated the cars lining
the cemetery road. Snow falling
on my father's death day, a little much
even to me, so prone to melancholy,

which is a way of skitching your loss.
Years ago, I had a friend, who used to say
love is a kind of opening.
She had a freezer stashed with vodka
and chocolate, a way of making me crash
on her couch. My friend was talking
about trees, what we know, what we feel,
how they conspire each other.
I was afraid then that if I stopped by
and listened long enough my body
would fly open, a blizzard of wings.
I thought that if I gave up grieving,
even one night, he'd die all over again,
or I'd die without something to grieve.
She must've known this too,
how winter shuts a mouth down,
then more mouth, more mouth.
Some days, the light right, I walk
an hour or so into a stand of birches
not far from my house, move through
the space between trees, and it's like
the trees pass through me, the ghost
of my breath, my father, my friend
sitting on the couch in her apartment.
We are all there. I hear them talking
and want to slip off my shoes—
Snow, listening, the nerve to stay awhile,
it's exactly like she was saying.

ARS POETICA
Corey Van Landingham

In the sad little garden
of William Paca, where the period
roses have been yanked out
for refusing their modern soil,
the nearby holly bushes are nothing
but restraint—pruned
and placed between the cement
path's spokes. From a window,
one can view the geometric designs
demonstrating what control
humans have over the pear tree,
the errant hibiscus blooming hot
in late October. "It seems to me,"
Keats wrote in a letter, "that we should rather
be the flower than the bee."
That we should rather receive, not take,
the world. I should not ask
for your good mouth
in the morning but find it with pleasant
surprise, perfect repose.
And your being above me, glorious
in this light, over my head, should make me
a mortal that falls back to gaze on you.
Consider Simone, sitting

in Toulouse's garden, bathed in sunlight,
where everything was agreeable.
"This fine weather, these flowers, this charming
little house." She felt "quite softened."
Signed each letter with a little
kiss and waited years to hold again
Jean-Paul's little arm.
And we, who are not unlike the garden,
who have our own sad history, are given
the language of past lovers who acted
out their roles. More light and light
it grows, the pears so ripe
they drop and rot,
slick, sun-opened. Shall I
so govern sentiment?
Wake and watch the tourists
shuffle by, contain myself
to not reach out and touch them?
Love, I am not ashamed. How I prefer
to tell you exactly what I want.

THE NARCISSIST
Wayne Miller

Our boats on the black water, and the lighthouse
swinging its gaze around, its beam
reaching and withdrawing, reaching
and withdrawing. It seemed
as though the whole sea rose up
to that towering eye.

                                    It seemed as though
it might have the power
to draw us from our shadows,
to lure us toward the rocks the waves
were breaking hard against. What would we do
if we got there?

                                  But we were farther
away than we'd supposed—and when that blaze
of light slid briefly across us
it only served to show us to each other.

HANSEL AND GRETEL IN REVERSE
Dara Yen Elerath

When the witch pulled us from the oven, we were beautiful, Hansel. Our hair turned from cinders to flaxen strands, our skin thickened, sweaters knitted themselves across our chests, wooden shoes cooled and hardened on our feet. Yet, we had to leave that house of gingerbread and licorice. We stumbled backwards through the forest, pained to see the witch's face grow distant. Brother, do you remember? Breadcrumbs flew up to your palms like birds, they formed a loaf of sourdough round and thick as the moon. Mother, I heard you scream as we blundered blindly through night-thickets, through cracked ribs of trees. Now, in this new house, with this new family, our bodies grow smaller. Hansel, what enchantment have they wrought on us? At dinner, the woodcutter pulls blood sausage from his lips and the wife turns it into a pig. I fear she is preparing us for something. Note the delight she takes in brushing dirt onto our faces, in removing clothes from our bodies and placing them in oaken drawers. Between her legs there is the scent of something terrible, the scent of a graveyard. At night, in my dreams, I still hear the buckle of the witch's belt clattering, that rattle of our infancy. Brother, let's go back. I miss the cage and flame, the witch's palms stained with ash, the way her knuckles rapped our knees as she appraised our bodies, turning them back and forth to check the fat; this, a thing that every loving mother does.

I WON'T LIE
Jennifer Wheelock

At 3 a.m. Dad wants to pick the strawberries. Outside the season
is wrong, the trees a tangle of twigs against a brain-gray sky. I won't lie:
If we're going to speak of strawberries, Mom and I would like him to be
calm, like the man at the roadside stand—the one Dad wandered
into that time he left the house on foot. The man at the roadside stand is measured
when he calls to say Dad is there fumbling the fruit. The man is silent
when we arrive. For months he disappears into his fields of blossoms and buzz,
then shows up with punnets of berries, preserves, chewing tobacco, a lifted chin.
At 5 a.m. Dad wants a gun. He says over and over and over and over
how if only he had a pistol he could shoot himself, himself who is no longer
himself but who is standing beside his own road trying to get back. I won't lie:
If we could, Mom and I would place the pistol, gently as we'd place
a too-ripe plum, into his hand.

THE CHILD PUTS APPLES INTO THE MOUTH OF THE TREE
Claire Wahmanholm

After we lost the child, a hole appeared between your lungs. At first it was the size of a gasp, an apple, a fist. Then it widened into the size of a plate, a small face. We had read about this sort of thing happening: after a bad grief, the heart goes bad and turns on the body, sucking everything into it like a spillway. *Look,* you said one day. You put your hand to the edge of the hole and the tips of your fingers vanished. You put your hand in up to your wrist and pulled back the emptiest fist. I was in the middle of dying, but I pulled myself from the dirt and bent before your chest and looked. Instead of the mesh of your body, instead of the room behind you, I saw a black meadow. Warm wind breathing against my skin. I hadn't thought there would be wind. I hadn't thought there would be anything. That night I dreamed of our child in that black meadow, dropping apples into the hollow of a dead tree. Her hands put apple after apple into the mouth of the tree and came back whole. So it was possible. I could feel her breath on each apple as she held it toward me. The meadow rippled with it. When I woke up I reached out in the dark to make sure you hadn't disappeared without me. When you do, I want you to take my hand.

THEY CALLED IT THE PARLOR
Meghann Plunkett

but it was just a small, sectioned off square of linoleum–a mock-room
    made with thick, hospital-blue curtains swooping open and closed
        like a school play, whooshing women in and out with a metallic

whir. We were there to release the slow sludge of anesthesia
    from of our eyes. Ushered inside to recline in a chair matted
        with a waterproof sheen. Polyester groaning and the weight

of a body mid-bleed, an inch of cotton pressed between our legs.
    Lit like a supermarket, five of us wreathed into a circle of bright loss.
        A thin paper gown pulled down as I tucked my knees

into the cramping. One woman pulled a curl from her head and let it snap
    back, snap back with the buzz of the fluorescents. Another thumbed
        through the worn pages of a Bible, mumbling a silent prayer.

The attempt to make it appear as though it were a living-room uneased me.
    A side table nesting a small plastic plant, a staged coffee table
        in the center and a bowl of waxed apples. A nurse swooped

in now and again to take our temperatures with a sheathed thermometer
    like a hummingbird trying to feed from our mouths. We opened
        and closed our jaws like clock toys. A check next

to each of our names, we waited—silent as a blackout. Let me never forget
how each of us, learning how to stand again, shifted our weight
from foot to foot in slip-free, neon socks. Each of us holding

a little pouch of wafers to bring our blood-sugar up. And the woman with
a port-wine stain covering one eye. How she leaked penny-sized
breastmilk stains and breathed into her hands, palming

her mascara into long, grey streaks. And how the nurse leaned down to tell her
that the man she came with needed to know   *how much longer?*
Let me never forget the way her body bucked

in response. Looking at me with disbelief. Let me never forget how we
laughed, shaking our heads, letting our hands touch.
In that room stinging with women, I sat there with her

in defiance.   *Let him wait.*

NOTICE OF RISKS
Corinna McClanahan Schroeder

The great bulk of novel readers are females; and to them such impressions (as are conveyed through fiction) are peculiarly mischievous: for, first, they are naturally more sensitive, more impressionable, than the other sex; and secondly, their engagements are of a less engrossing character—they have more time as well as more inclination to indulge in reveries of fiction.
—"Moral and Political Tendency of the Modern Novels," *Church of England Quarterly Review* (1842)

Once, when she was reading, a paper nest of wasps buzzed between her ears / Once, when she was reading, a fishing knife sliced open her gleaming / hair curling in the humid words / Once, she slipped free of her body like an omniscient fog / Once, fingertips throbbed / Once, when she was reading, her brother ripped the book in two / Once, the story's rain ruined her cheeks and shoes / Once, her book locked behind glass / father holding the key / Once, when she was reading, the sugar of syllables crunched between her teeth / Once, she wandered lost through brambles and thorns / Once, snow drifts heaped in her bones / Once, thighs to chest: *let her go let her go let her go* / Once, when she was reading, her mother burned the book / a flare, then a smoldering / Once, when she was reading, her body was a wool coat and she could not swim in its weight / Once, she slipped her book / inside another book to keep it safe / Once, she spit out the words like sour wine / Once, an easterly wind blew from inside / Once, when she was reading, early flowers rose on the fields of her arms / Once, there was only blight / Once, she was a sopping sheet wrung dry

BOY
Maya Pindyck

Someone made the school a plaque
of names. I find the one I wanted

for my never-son: bronze prince
stirring a pond with all his brothers.

My family came here from a country
I am not allowed to visit

even though its spices fill my cabinet.
My other family never made it.

I once walked a field
covering their bodies. Wildflowers

& grasses. Here, the story of a line
of children shot in the schoolyard.

Here, Manek's hairbrush shop.
What I can't wrap my head around

is the story of the boy playing ball
by the hole where they hid—

how he ratted them out to a soldier.
I try to imagine how that boy

grew. To love his own
boys, only, playing hide & seek

in the sun? And is that boy's boy
a boy who now trains to turn

a life lethal, to pull a trigger
out of fear, or rage, or duty?

I don't know, but I think it's the same boy
stammering history & now & here—boy

who waves in the night to be seen.

VIRTUE SIGNALING
Tiana Clark

You couldn't know this loneliness . . .
—Natalie Eilbert

My first night in Madison   the air was different—
cool, less sticky. The street   was quiet, weirdly   stagnant.

Our house, a pale yellow. I straddled the   isthmus,
felt ice chip   between both lakes   like frozen lace.

I'm hyper   visible now,   so seen, so   everywhere, then suddenly
nowhere—so much so, I became   Muzak   to my own face.

Now   I'm being followed   inside a grocery store. Down each aisle,
then back again. Now I'm being   stalked   inside a restaurant.

I switch seats.   But it does not matter. I feel it all: the eyeballs
of this town scorch   the back of my neck,   skin already darker there.

I want to pluck   all the signs   I see stapled across
these manicured lawns   that read: Black Lives Matter.

I don't believe you.   There is a sign you buy because
you want so badly to believe   in what it has to say,

and then there is a sign you buy   because
you want others to believe you are brave.

A sign can't save   my life?   You will not spare me.
I watch   as you watch me   I watch

as my white students watch me   I watch me   watch me, smaller now
than when I first moved here.   Lost a quarter of an inch

my doctor said.   Most days   I wait
for the bitter winter to end.   Most days   I wait   for another black

person to pass me.   Most days   they never come.
Most days I wait   for another black person   to save me

and we hold the gaze.   We do not smile or lie.   A simple nod
simply   saves my life.

DRIVING THROUGH WYOMING, LISTENING TO THE RADIO
Sophie Klahr

Burrs, creeks, elms. . . .   here are some more things I like:
the words *antidote* and *thistle*. Embers.
Each pillaged and blown-out motel along
state roads. How someone in a parking lot
asks how much I want for the faded globe
in my passenger seat. *The world,* I say.
How it seems the town where a young man was
crucified all those years ago became
gentle. The idea of deep time is
that we keep nothing, it just is what it
is. *It is what it is*—this too I like.
The friar's idea of The One Sadness.
God shed America—the boy being
dragged, naked: the body all our bodies.

VARIATION ON A THEME BY GIL SCOTT-HERON
John Murillo

Near midnight mid-December,
and my junkie uncle, the soldier,
   sleepwalks home. Up avenues
strewn with everyday debris,
   past rats he imagines man-made
and robot. In his heavy half sleep,
   he palms, barely, a bone knife stolen
from the dead butcher's meatshop.
   Gris-gris against the bandits
in his head, the hounds at his heels.
   There's a rumble, now, rising
from behind the old armory.
   A black chopper lifting,
lighting up the block. It hovers
   like a hummingbird bred for death.
When he points it out to passersby,
   they laugh or look away. He points
again, of course it's gone. The one
   good cloud he can still make out
is where his god resides. That's
   the good news. The bad news
is that his god has got three trained
   snipers beaming from a rooftop.
In each one's crosshairs, uncle soldier

ducks and staggers. Early winter,
his breath is bonedust. Decorated
war dog whose only friends are ghosts.
But even they, tonight, are elsewhere.

DRIVING THROUGH KANSAS AT NIGHT
David Keplinger

Why must some sorrows go on forever,
The grief you can't let go of
Like the piece of broken furniture
In which you kept your first books,

Or the moon that follows brightly
Through clouds on route 70 while somewhere
Someone is still suffering, remembering again
The illness they'll have to get up

And look at again in the mirror.
Coleman Hawkins plays Body and Soul
For the ten millionth time and it is still good:
So it continues playing on this station

For as long as it stays good, as the corn mills
Stream by through small towns like clouds,
And the faces in the all night restaurants
Glance up as you pass.

FIRST WEDDING DANCE
Marcelo Hernandez Castillo

The music stopped playing years ago
but we're still dancing.

There's your bright skirt scissoring
through the crowd—

our hips tipping the instruments over.

You open me up and walk inside
until you reach a river
where a child is washing her feet.

You aren't sure
if I am the child
or if I am the river.

You throw a stone
and the child wades in to find it.
This is memory.

Let's say the river is too deep
so you turn around and leave
the same way you entered—
spent and unwashed.

It's ok. We are young, and
our gowns are as long as the room.

I told you I always wanted a silk train.

We can both be the bride,
we can both empty our lover.

And there's nothing different about you—
about me—about any of this.
Only that we wish it still hurt, just once.

Like the belts our fathers whipped us with,
not to hurt us but just to make sure we remembered.

Like the cotton ball, dipped in alcohol,
rubbed gently on your arm
moments before the doctor asks you to breathe.

FROM MOTHERSALT: A LYRIC
Mia Ayumi Malhotra

37 weeks, 1 day

If the body goes rogue, turns against itself. If between breaths, all I hear is the crunch of body against brick. If I am both body and brick. If I am broken and not remade. If this breath, stoppered in my throat, is a room without release. If I reach for the way out but do not find it. If you, too, are straining, fist against face, knees against torso, struggling to be free.

38 weeks, 6 days

I wake with a bullet between my teeth, grinning. The moon hangs in my hair like a flash of light. I am the body fantastic, dripping with silver and night sweats. A brilliant orb in the sky. Come near, I dare you, I am swollen with the bounty of fall. I crackle, I charge. My hair rises from the roots, a shower of sparks, gathered and scattered. Muscles lit with new fire, I throw my big-bellied challenge to the sky.

WAYS TO VIEW JOAN MIRÓ'S *TRIPTYCH BLEU, I, II, III*
Shannon K. Winston

1961

Start with the left
and you'll see rain on
a windshield after a storm.

Begin with the right,
you'll see only a kite string
drifting against the sky.

There are a thousand
ways to begin a story.
With the middle, perhaps,

is best: with a red sewing
needle stitching up black holes.
Or maybe they aren't

holes, but pebbles
skimming the water
seconds before they sink.

There are also a million ways
to interpret a story.
The way I took my lover's

silence for indifference.
The way she thought
my idle chatter was irreverence.

The way I sometimes
thought my sneaking to
her house in the middle

of the night was so lonely—
our secret rendezvous
collecting like black dots

against a blue canvas.
But then again,
how lovely the snow fell

all around me as I
trekked back and forth
between her house

and mine at midnight.
The sidewalk appeared
like black ovals

beneath
my feet where the snow
had melted. These

tiny openings.
How easy silence seemed.
Chosen, not imposed.

Like something
I could lean into,
like a simple red sliver.

A blot of paint. To
embroider, decorate.
To strip back, to cut.

Yes, maybe
this is the best
way in.

WORDS GAMES & SPACE TRAVEL
Shannon K. Winston

Michael Thompson, *Girl with a Hole in Her Stocking*, 2008

A hesitation. A hole. A rip.
    Sometimes, my thoughts

proceed like this. Like a teasing
    at the seams where one

thread loosens, then another
    only to contract in another

place. The way I think *splinter,*
    then *sister.* O' the association

games she and I played
    to pass the time. *Fall,*

she'd say. *Leaves,* I'd reply.
    Cotton candy, clouds.

Statement-response,
    syllables stitched up

the hours. *Almond, eye,*
    telescope.

Words aligned imperfectly,
    but that was the pleasure.

In the crevices and cracks,
      we sought out the ineffable.

What do you see?, I'd ask.
      A blue earring pulsing

in the baseboards.
      What do you feel?, her follow-up question.

My toe pushing through
      a rip in my stocking.

Bending down, I marveled at
      the smallest opening

widening, widening
      into ever-expanding present

where I feel grass, I feel bark,
      and leaves and linens

drying on clotheslines.
      Trampolines and hot air balloons.

Yellow wings (are they mine)?
      Here, the horizon is no thicker

than thread from which violet-
      blue beads hang,

tiny orbiting planets
      beneath my touch.

LOVE LETTER TO A STRANGER, WITH RAIN
Helena Mesa

Years ago, I read of an accident
in a country far from our own. The medics
arrived late, and as the ambulance
pulled from the curb, the crowd sang,
together, strangers making song
of an end many of us fear, and yet know
our bodies will meet in some way,
at some time. I'm saying this wrong.

This morning, a stillness—
a cabin and woods, miles and miles
but trees brushing shoulders and leaves,
and along one road, a swallowtail,
its ice-blue wings closing like a door.

Tell me how to reach you—which road
do I take, which swimming hole
will invite us, not stroke by stroke
along different shores, but where the spring
feeds from beneath and cools our feet.

When rain fell on the tin roof yesterday,
I thought I was in another country, the light
more aged than yellow. Let me hear you

tell stories, your voice a prayer
shedding light like stars after a storm.

Why wait until the siren resounds?
Why not sing like that now?

TO THE STRANGER UP NORTH
Helena Mesa

I'll never fit between your palms.
Go ahead, see me as the dying galaxy
your telescope seeks, your one eye
closed so all's gas and loss. I'm close,
but ninety miles can take days to cross
and water's hungrier than sharks.
My people leave, play house
in cities they decorate with bodegas
and pastel schools. Their children
speak last century's tongue,
study my curves on maps, and wait
for a border to open like a gate.
What sea respects walls, what walls
break the will of those living
on either side? Tunnel deeper, faster.
Rent a boat, sail closer to shore,
or not—I see you from here:
same storms, same parents
naming their daughters, same families
divided—same gravity, same anger—
each with her own madman
standing on the verandah and waving
his power like a child's toy.

YARDWORK
Keetje Kuipers

Every weekend I give you chores:
rake, fill feeders, give the grass a mow.
My body, too, is told to work, while yours—

lush and flowering on all scores—
is asked to wait for what mine might grow.
All week long I do my brand of chores,

priming the flesh's barren moors
with needled prescriptions designed to sow
these unnamed seeds that are not yours.

Making love some evening might restore
us to our freer former selves, though
touching could be one more chore

of prodding hands I've learned to ignore.
Now the nurses peck my limbs like crows,
discouraging my body's urge for yours—

I resist planting and can't bear play. But more
than plotted cycles, this I know:
Some things can't be fixed through faithful chores,
my body failing to work apart from yours.

GLASS BLOWER'S GLOSSARY
OF FLAWS AND DEFECTS
Keetje Kuipers

Small parison, slack and heavy bauble,
I breathed you into being with my want,

my belief in your fragile form I'd thought
to coax to life with pinpricks and prayers.

From my belly's furnace, I imagined
pulling you whole—beveled, and thinly

gilded with meconium's sharp-scented glaze.
Within my body's medicated light,

your molten form grew rivets and grooves, frit
coloring and clinging to your lucent bones,

lengths along which you might someday be touched.
When you refused conjuring, I carried

for months a dullness in my mouth, still not
knowing I had burnt my tongue on desire.

DIASPORA SONNET 51
Oliver de la Paz

I'm getting cold and the trees have darkened
from their green into a tobacco-colored stained.

The birds cease calling each other—
there are no more ears in the branches.

I haven't slept for two nights
because the silence skewers everything

with thought that cannot be broken. The depth
of my thinking drags all the drafts away

from my distractedness and from the weather
despite the rain and despite the commiseration of rain.

I've nothing here to monitor my selfhood—
Have their flung back heads exalted in the change?

Where have they gone? The birds and the finery
of their throats? Their limitless gratitude for seed and suet?

DIASPORA SONNET 54
Oliver de la Paz

Nettles for tea and the sore yesteryear awake
in the old calendar whose months have not turned—

and past the steam, the reflection of the ceiling fan
cuts at the syllables of story, saying *then, then, then*

each moment of being somewhere and someone
sliced into dimes. A little sugar can make this sweet

yet it's the pinprick of flavor that's keeping company.
Old hymns on the radio won't undo the way the body

is whittled by distance. Slice after slice this tether
severed until there's nothing but tea and afternoon news

and the lying months in their effacement. Spiral
bound but absent-minded like real memories,

the crossed off days until losing count and interest.
The broth on the lips, numbing till the words don't come.

NONFICTION

NOT BEAUTIFUL
Rick Kempa

There's this sorry-looking guy manning the self-checkout lane at the grocery store on Christmas morning. I glance at him as we walk by—stooped shoulders and drooping arms, unbuttoned sleeves and loose shirt-tail—and I say to Fern, "I guess Santa didn't give him what he wanted." She pokes me. "Hush!" Later, from the corner of the coffee bar at the front of the store, I eye him.

He leans on the counter with one balled hand, raps the surface with the other. He shifts his weight from side to side, one untied lace flapping. His forehead is a barrens strafed by winds, his mouth a small round cave, his eyes dull pebbles submersed in shallow, shifting pools. He licks his lips, rubs his palms across his pate.

Oh, the shoppers are bright today, a steady stream of good cheer, of Santa hats and tasseled scarves, a red and gold and green blur streaming through the checkout lanes! They wave at him when they need help, big looping gestures that one might use to catch a friend's eye in the street. He advances, looms above them, stabs some buttons on the screen, retreats. Their smiles fade, their thanks stick in their throats.

He's got a box of candy canes he has been told to give away. Such punishment! He tries to slip them in the sacks unseen. A girl in a reindeer suit extends a pudgy hand; he thrusts one at her and she ducks behind her mother's skirt.

A woman with a gold wreath emblazoned on a black sweatshirt does not go quietly. "Merry Christmas!" she barks, and shows her teeth. He cringes as if slapped, and she mocks him as she flows past in a sing-song way: ". . . or whatever it is that you say on this day."

He will say nothing. A single word or half a breath might breach the dam. What is it? Schism? Loss?

■ ■ ■

Here at my table in the corner with my coffee and notebook and pen, and my body folded into itself, eyes narrowed, forehead creased—apparently I too seem an object of suffering, because the people in line for their Christmas drink are trying to catch my eye so they can assail my gloom. A young woman in a sweat suit waiting for her drink sidles up, says soberly, "Good morning, sir." I must remind her of her father.

It's true, I'm hurting suddenly for this man unmoored in the checkout lane and for all to whom I am no help: my daughter's ex-boyfriend, a good guy, alone today with his video games in this very town; my brother standing at our parents' graves in Denver, talking to them as if they are all gathered around the kitchen table; the estranged son of another brother in his cheap flat in Brooklyn; the uncounted others out in the street the way I was one Christmas decades back, hearing the laughter and songs and surprised shrieks spill from the tenement houses—"Aw ma, you shouldn't have!" "Come here child, so I can hug you." In my pocket were just enough coins for a drink or a phone call, and I walked all morning fingering them because I did not know which I needed most.

Worst of all was this: a man wrestling with a Christmas tree by a dumpster. It was bigger than him, and it fought back. The boughs caught and rode the wind like tinseled sails, and it rose from his hands and bounced on the gravel, once, twice. He scuttled after it. I wanted to say, "Hey man, what's the rush? It's eight a.m. on Christmas Day!" I thought of the children in his home staring at its absence. But dumpster space must be seized, or lost. He gripped the trunk and a clump of boughs, rocked back on his heels, and heaved it at the bin. It landed with a *whoosh* and exhaled the last of the warm air from his living room, and we turned from it, a thing unloved and thus not beautiful.

AIR DOG
Rebecca Childers

My mom craved pizza. She called my dad's parents to see if they wanted some. It was summer; all four of my mom's children were home from college and we wanted pizza, too. Waiting for an update on lunch, we hung out by the phone while she talked to our grandmother. Our mother said a quick hello, listened, and then gasped into the phone, "How long do you think he has?" My little brother, Joshua, grabbed my hand and squeezed. Our mother hung up and said, "It's your grampa's brother, Uncle Everett. He showed up at their house last night, half out of his head. Told them he was fixing to die in the next couple of days. Your grandma says he looks it."

We snapped into crisis mode. All six of us hopped into my parents' minivan and headed across the river to say goodbye. My grandmother greeted us at the door, relieved us of our pizza boxes, and led us to the dining room, shouting the whole way there. "Poor thing, peed the bed straight through. Yep, I've lost eight siblings now—dear God! —and I know the look of one about to meet their maker. I figured we could give him a good place to die." We tried to get her to lower her voice, but it was useless. "Everett won't be able to hear me unless I shout it in his ear," she said. But we knew our grandmother. She wouldn't have been quiet if he'd had perfect hearing.

The pizza lured him out of bed. Unable to handle the sudden fragility of our beloved uncle, my brother made a beeline for the door when he saw Everett, vacating a seat at the head of the table. Wrapped in four layers of blankets, Everett sat down and ate a piece of supreme with his left hand. His right arm hung beside him, with his palm cupping air and slowly rocking back and forth. "You patting a dog there, Uncle Everett?" my sister asked, unsure what to say. He ignored her so my grandmother shouted the question into his ear. Then his neck straightened up, his hazy eyes became their old piercing blue.

"I'm petting Jack," Everett said, now affectionately scratching his air dog's ears with both hands. "When I was still in my mother, Jack stood guard by her, growling at anyone who put a hand on her, even just to touch her belly. Then, when I was born, he slept beside my crib. I guess he decided he was my protector." Here Everett paused to lightly chuckle and run a hand all the way down the air dog's back. "Yep, he protected me then and he protects now," he said.

Three days after we ate pizza with Everett and Jack, my grandparents decided they could no longer care for Everett alone and checked him into the hospital to die. The hospital released him a week later. He went back to his house and kept on living. Nobody mentioned it, but I'm sure, that in that hospital room with the beeping boxes and the chaplain leading Everett in a reading of his final Psalm, Jack kept watch.

I am starting to think that the dead never really go away.

■ ■ ■

My dad and I believe that you can have any number of animals that you love in your lifetime, and that love you, but you only get one life-dog. This dog shares your soul. When you hurt, it hurts; when it hurts, you hurt. Everett's life-dog was Jack. My dad's life-dog was a fifteen-inch Beagle named Bud. My dad, David, named him Bud, at six, because he wanted a dog to be his bud.

When Bud was a few years old, he decided to go joyriding with David's dad on his way to work. His dad didn't notice the dog in the backseat until he was a few blocks away from home. He opened the car door and let Bud out. These details came out fifty years after the fact. All little David knew was that his bud was missing.

About a week later, David's family drove by Bud, miraculously inside a fence, a few blocks away from their house. David screamed *stop*, climbed the fence, got Bud, and climbed back out. Now, my dad says he should have knocked on the door. He should have talked to the people who had been taking care of the wandering beagle. But at the time all he knew was he saw his dog, and he was getting his dog back.

When David first brought Bud home, he built a dog house with a wooden fence around it. Bud got out. Then David helped his father build a fence around the whole backyard. Bud climbed the boards like a ladder. So David tied him to a tree with a chain. Bud wiggled his legs back and forth, back and forth, until he wore links of the chain out. David made a chicken wire pen. Bud got out. Finally tied to a chain, surrounded by a chicken wire pen, inside of the wooden fence, Bud stayed in.

Bud never went far when he escaped. He just wanted freedom. He liked to listen for the scrape of the metal door of the storage shed on cool summer mornings. This sound meant my dad and his two brothers were heading out to fish by the river. Bud would follow at their heels, detouring occasionally to chase muskrats and rabbits.

A large wall of grass covered dirt protects Huntington from the Ohio River, and my dad and his brothers lived at the foot of it. Walking on the floodwall allowed David to reach Camden Park, West Virginia's only amusement park, in a matter of minutes. At that time, it was also a zoo; local residents were lulled to sleep by the roar of the sad lion. David journeyed there to pat the horses the park kept in stables outside the gates. He only went when he felt brave, though. A mean boxer liked to hang out there. One day with treats for the horses in his pockets, David meandered down to the stables with Bud. The boxer came out of nowhere, growling at the little boy. The Boxer ran towards them. Bud threw his small body under the charging dog. The Boxer flew through the air and landed on his back, okay, but stunned and scared.

Fifty years later, my dad and I walked down the floodwall together. He pointed to a tree he'd climbed at fifteen to place a blue rubber ball in a knot at the top. He wondered if the tree had accepted it, and grown around it on its ascent to the sky. I'd never heard this story and watched closely as my dad used his hands to explain to me how much the tree had grown. This wasn't one of the important stories, one of the stories that he felt his children had to know to understand him. Like the story of Bud, his Beagle who was never far away. I knew these stories so well they felt like my stories. Bud had been my dad's protector, so in a way, that made him mine, too. The day my dad told me about the ball in the tree, we wandered off our usual path, accidentally entering the territory of a growling Rottweiler. It ran towards us. "Stay still," my dad said, calm. We stood still. The Rottweiler stopped running and stared. Then, inexplicably, it darted away. "I bet Bud got him," he said to me, laughing. "I bet he did," I said, laughing, too. What we didn't say out loud was that neither of us worried as the dog ran towards us, teeth bared. We never doubted that the dog would decide it best to turn and run.

■ ■ ■

Observing Uncle Everett patting his air dog was not the first time Jack had entered into family legend. My dad had grown up with the story of Jack and the ditch. One day, when my grampa, Everett's older brother, was walking home from his one room school house, two guys came out of the woods with guns. They pointed them at my grandfather. "Get him," one said to the other with a nudge of his elbow. But Jack had come to walk Grampa home from school. He emerged from of a patch of nearby trees and began to growl at the armed men. The giant black German Shepherd snarled, erasing all thought of the blond little boy. "Let's get the dog," they said. They turned their weapons on Jack and pulled the trigger, but Jack spotted a crude drainage ditch by the side of the road. He hopped in and crawled on his belly all the way home, keeping himself safe, while distracting the bullies from his young master.

When it came time for my dad to get his second dog, he figured he needed an angle to convince his dad. He thought back to the stories of Jack the German Shepherd and scoured the newspaper. "German Shepherd-Pure breed, No papers," it said. David's dad took him down to look at the litter. They picked out the runt, a little black male, and named him Ben. Like Clifford the Big Red Dog, Ben grew big and strong, over twenty-eight inches at the shoulder, over one hundred pounds.

Around this time, my grandmother started to get lonely for female companionship. She had three sons, a husband, and a giant boy dog. A stray mutt knocked up the neighbor's beagle, and my grandmother got to view the puppies first. Suzy pranced around in her white fur, interrupted by brown patches. Black stripes ran across the brown. My grandma lifted her out of the neighbor's yard and sat her down inside her own. Suzy became Ben's shadow, following his massive paws everywhere. If someone came by the yard, Ben stood by Suzy like a big brother.

A big mutt spotted Suzy in the yard one day. By herself, happily lying in a sun beam, she looked weak and easy to pick on. The dog barreled over to Suzy and growled. She jumped up, howled, and ran. He chased her, snapping at her little paws with his giant teeth. Then Ben, who had been seeing to business elsewhere, heard Suzy's cries. Within seconds of his arrival, Ben knocked the mutt down with his paws, picked him up by the belly and shook him like a rag doll. When Ben set the mutt down, the dog scurried away. My dad watched all this from the kitchen window.

A week later, my dad saw that mutt again. It was running down the street, frightened. Except this time, it wasn't Ben, but Suzy who chased him. "Was she all by herself?" I asked my dad when he first told me this story. "Yes, all alone," he said. "So the dog was scared of her without Ben there?" I asked. "Oh, Ben was there. He might have been invisible, but to Suzy and to that mutt, Ben was there." You don't have to be present to be with someone. I don't think it is possible to completely leave those we love.

■ ■ ■

I often trace the history of my family by thinking through our dogs. When my parents just had my two oldest sisters, they got a white terrier from the animal shelter named Scruffy. It ran away not long after they got it. When I was little, my oldest sister claimed she had loved it anyway. I didn't understand why. Scruffy had no loyalty.

The first family dog I met was a Beagle-mix named Kenny. While I was growing up, my mother threatened to write a book about getting Kenny called,

"Mommy's pregnant, time to get another dog." The kid she was pregnant with was me.

Kenny stars in one of my family's favorite stories. My sister, Jennifer, the little sister until I came around, once huffed around the kitchen, finally sitting down on Kenny's back. "I had to sit on the puppy, cause I didn't have a seat," she said to defend herself. Kenny yelped, but he soon forgave her. She and my oldest sister walked around the neighborhood with him, picking sour grass and throwing birthday parties for all of the neighborhood dogs.

In a home video, my mother pretends to search for my sister. She points her video camera outside. "Jennifer, where are you?" her disembodied voice shouts, a bit too close to the camera's microphone. Kenny pops out of a little dog house, the one my dad made out of a gutted TV. The next to emerge: the creature we affectionately called Slobberdog. Then two more dogs come out of the tiny hole. "Wow, that is a lot of dogs in there," my mother says. She begins to laugh as my sister crawls out of the doghouse on her hands, stands up, wipes her palms on her knees and waves to the camera. "I hope I don't have to pay them for babysitting," my mom jokes.

■ ■ ■

Kenny died tragically and far too young. Before his death, my sisters and I had never seen our dad cry. I was five, and we had to find a new dog. On the way to fly kites at the park, we passed a sign that read "Beagle, Gun Dog." The tiny gun dog had green eyes and basset-hound-length ears. We named her Kassie.

When I think of my family, all six of us living together in the small brown house, I think of Kassie, too. My dad never thought much of her beagle-ness. To him, Bud was the beagle. But he still walked Kassie on the floodwall he'd walked Bud on, and he let her sniff rabbit trails by that same river.

Kassie was the matriarch of our pets. When our rabbit broke her leg and hopped onto Kassie's bed for a nap, extending her long cast covered leg as far as it would go, Kassie slept on the ground next to her. When my family decided to bring two starving kittens home, the kittens found the holes in the cover of

Kassie's foam bed and hid there. While she slept, they slid their paws out of hiding and swung Kassie's ears and flipped her tail up and down. Kassie opened one eye, rolled it, and went back to sleep.

My brother and I didn't always love dogs. My mother had gates put on the back deck so I wouldn't be scared to go outside. Joshua often followed my lead, so he didn't care much for dogs, either. Joshua and I always gave Kassie food we didn't like and a pat now and then, but she wasn't ever the reason we were happy to be home. So, when it came time to say our goodbyes to Kassie, we were surprised by how much it hurt. She lay on her bed in the living room floor, covered in blankets. My sisters administered Gatorade to her through a turkey baster every few hours and changed her pee pads. Joshua and I sat in the kitchen with pillows covering our ears in an effort to not hear her wheezes. I wrote some bad poetry.

"Where are the people/ with the casseroles?" I read out loud.

Joshua whispered to me, "This is the most I've ever liked someone who died."

■ ■ ■

A week before my brother Joshua died, tragically and far too young, he laid out for me his elaborate plan to steal the neighbor's dog. He'd formed a bond with the Scotty-mix during his midnight walks to buy packs of Marlboros. The dog, Raider, would wear a bandana for disguise, his shaggy gray fur dyed yellow. "That's the only dog I could see myself really loving, Rebecca," he said, "besides Brownie, of course." Joshua loved temporary things. Wanderers. In his twenty-two years, he only had one pet he called his own. The mutt with German shepherd coloring that Joshua lovingly referred to as Brownie introduced himself to our family during dinner when Joshua was about nine years old. Brownie put his wet nose on our glass back door, poked out his tongue and started to lick the shiny surface. Ignoring the whines of the fat Beagle in the kitchen and the protests of our mother, Joshua picked up the strips of roast he'd been stirring into the mashed potatoes on his plate, opened the door, and dropped them in Brownie's open mouth.

Brownie became Joshua's friend after that. He'd drop by when he was in the neighborhood. Brownie didn't have an owner. My family hypothesized that when Brownie started to walk, he couldn't stop. Our dad had called him Nomad, until Joshua christened him Brownie. We spotted Brownie all over our town, sometimes a forty-five-minute car ride from our house. Always on a mission. We tried to keep him, several times. Once he limped to our backdoor with a hole bitten through his leg. My parents sat in an emergency room all night, using our bill money to get him ten stitches. Brownie chewed them off. A week later, he turned up with new stitches. He'd been neutered. My family realized we weren't the only people who wanted him that he didn't want back. Despite Brownie's shaky allegiance, Joshua still jumped up and down every time he saw him. They greeted each other like cruelly separated best friends, snuggling for hours on the back porch. The unstable nature of Joshua's life-dog always worried me.

■ ■ ■

I met my life-dog in a ditch on the way to history class my sophomore year in college. I'd left my parents' house an hour early in hopes of running into my new boyfriend in the cafeteria. On the winding road, by the gas plant, about two minutes from my parents' house, I slammed on my brakes when a black dog darted across the road. I pulled over and got out. I told myself I was just check-ing to make sure it wasn't injured. When I walked to the side of the road, I saw that it had crawled into a drainage pipe. "Puppy," I shouted. It growled back. I looked down at the drainage pipe; it was at the end of a very steep ditch. I knew I would need some help to climb down, get the dog, and climb back up. "I have to go to class," I told it. "But after that I'll come back with my sister. I promise."

I called my dad from school and told him about the dog. I told him about the growl, how I figured it either had puppies or rabies. He thought back to my days of darting under the minivan to escape a harmless St. Bernard. "Leave it to the professionals, Rebecca," he said. I told him I would. I went to the same school as my sister, Jennifer. When she got out of class, we checked the ditch. The dog was still there. We coaxed it out with a bag of Cheetos. It was a small puppy, a smooth-haired Border Collie mix. We put him in on our car and took him home, letting him have free rein of the back yard. When my dad drove up he admonished me for getting the dog, then said, "Why isn't there a collar and a leash on him? He might leave."

I believe that Charlie, the Border Collie, waited in the ditch for me because I'd made him a promise. I honestly don't know why I did. When I saw the flash of black cross the street, I instinctively followed it. Charlie and I have the same mind. We worry. I have to leave him at my parent's house with their big yard, but when I come home he nips my ankles, angry for a minute, then we dance together with glee. The day my brother left us, we once again entered family crisis mode, pulling out the minivan to collect everybody. That night no one slept, but we all lay in our beds for a little while with our eyes closed. I tried, but Charlie wouldn't let me. He poked me with his nose until I followed him. One by one, we went to each person's room. We watched them breathe for a minute and then moved on. Then we made our rounds again. When I tried to sit down, Charlie cried. So all night, we circled the house, watching people in their beds. The next day I told my dad.

"I guess he's worried about us," I said. "No, Rebecca, he's a herding dog. He thinks he's lost one of his sheep."

■ ■ ■

My sister, Jennifer, likes to order eggs off the internet. Once she hatched a family of quail in our living room. Together, the hatchlings planned a breakout, the eight of them scattered. One pooped on my grandfather's picture. Another on my mother's lace curtains. A few years after this, a turkey egg came unexpectedly in the mail. Probably a gift from the company: "Here, have a free turkey, then order from us again." We hatched the turkey and gave him to a man who often saw wild turkeys on his farm. The turkey egg arrived in a box with layers of cushiony foam. We left this box, open and forgotten, on our deck long after the birth of the turkey. Soon, an old Beagle about nine with almost no teeth, bald spots, and sagging nipples from yet another batch of puppies claimed the box as her bed and slept there every night. Her family had moved out of our neighborhood, abandoning her. Kassie's death had left an old beagle-sized hole in our hearts. We welcomed the new old Beagle. She and Charlie became bosom buddies. We named her Sally. Charlie believed Sally when she told him they needed to howl at trees or chase leaves like they were rabbits. Sally believed she had to keep an eye on our perimeter. Protect us.

Sally was not like any dog we had ever met. She'd had enough of wandering. When she found that box, she refused to leave. Without a leash or a fence, she stayed. Charlie and I liked to spend summer mornings walking around the neighborhood. Sally spent hers sitting on the back porch, watching the neighbors leave for work. When Sally saw us leaving, she stood up, stretched her short arthritic legs and followed us down the driveway. We often met Joshua on these walks, on his way back from a cigarette run, the neighbor's dog, Raider, following closely behind him. We'd take a few laps together. Then we'd all go back up the driveway. Charlie and I went inside the house, Raider turned around and headed home, and Sally sat at Joshua's side on the porch steps while he smoked. She refused to come in the house until we all were inside with her. After Joshua died, Charlie and I still took these walks. Sally toppled down the driveway behind us, and Raider, coming from the direction of the gas station, met us mid-walk. After several laps, we all headed up the driveway together. Charlie and I went inside, Raider went home, and Sally sat on the porch steps for a while. After the length of a cigarette, Sally tapped her nails on the glass door, wanting to come in.

I'VE LIVED LONG ENOUGH
Jim Natal

I've lived long enough to see the Bible proven wrong. The rich have inherited the earth. Remember the bestselling myth of *The Millionaire Next Door*? Forget it. Ever seen the old black-and-white TV show *The Millionaire* in which some fictional down-and-outer was given a check for a million dollars, tax free, by rich guy Michael Anthony? Chump change. Speaking of television, *The Six Million Dollar Man* from the 1970s is being re-booted as, what else, *The Six Billion Dollar Man*. In other words, worth is measured in billions now. Powerball tickets, too. When was the last time you heard about a corporate merger, a start-up buyout, with a figure in the millions? Any CEO mogul, hedge fund manager, ruthless dictator, international criminal, App creator, or Super PAC mega-donor worth his pink sea salt has nine zeros in his Panamanian/Cayman (previously Swiss) bank account. Of course, life is not all roses and cherry bowls for billionaires. It's as hard to park all that cash (legit or not) as it is to find an unpermitted space on a Santa Monica side street. Now that bank laundries are under close scrutiny, I hear Miami high-rise condos are being bought and gambled like casino chips. Shrewd move . . . until sea levels rise, and those investments are deeper underwater than a middle-class mortgage.

Elephants, blue whales,
Himalayan mountain peaks
Too big to fail

CLIMATE CHANGE NAYSAYERS
Jim Natal

Climate change naysayers. Unproven science. Fake news. The sky is falling down in flames. The hottest year on record worldwide and the new year promises to be hotter yet. But don't sweat it. This has all happened before and we survived, didn't we? So what if Phoenix and furnace are now interchangeable terms? So what if the polar caps are melting like ice chips in a Happy Hour margarita? Oh, and ignore those ceaseless firestorms and tropical storms, that 70-mile crack in the Antarctic glacier that calved like a gargantuan white cow. Repeat after me and a sage Oklahoma senator, along with an actual climate scientist (who also believes smoking doesn't cause lung cancer): global warming isn't real and it's not our fault. Why make a volcano out of a molehill? Trust us—97 percent of the world's scientists *can* be wrong.

> Dandelion clocks
> So much for humanity
> Dries up, blows away

TRANSLATION

TWO POEMS
Lidija Dimkovska

translated by

Ljubica Arsovska and Patricia Marsh Stefanovska

HUMP

In front of me a man is pushing
a barrow full of empty plastic bottles.
The path is narrow, I can't overtake him.
I follow him, watch him.
Worn-out trousers,
furrowed hands,
a pair of mismatched slippers,
and under the ragged T-shirt
      —a hump, marked with pain
as with a Star of David.
He's the same age as me,
of a time long past.
In vain has he memorized
the short poems about the fatherland,
unnecessary like theory learned by heart
but never put into practice in this world
where today he has
neither father nor fatherland.
Has someone underwritten his life
in black and white,
or do only these bottles rate him among the living?
The bottles bounce,

he leans into the rhythm of the barrow,
I hear his stomach rumble,
and a sigh escapes his mouth.
The path is long, we tread one behind the other,
I in the beat of his gait,
he in the cadence of the three wheels.
I feel that out of my heavy-heartedness,
from the uneasiness of my senses,
hope, future and aim evaporate,
the liquids leach out of my organs,
the air is squeezed out, my weight dissipates,
I no longer have content,
I'm turning into an empty plastic bottle
that gets smaller and smaller and then throws itself
among the other bottles,
I take the least room in the cart,
and the man, sinking into his own deepest place,
only now begins to sweat,
wipes his face first with one hand then with the other
while the barrow topples
and he stops, takes off his T-shirt
and dabs the streams of sweat running down his neck,
turns his head left and right,
but sees no one behind him,
only the tip of his own hump,
marked with pain as with the Star of David.

BEHIND THE DOOR

When I took the gun off the nail,
the cracked plaster behind the door crumbled,
an imprint of emptiness opened up in the patch.
How many people can one kill with it?
And how many without pressing the trigger?
In a dream, or with a curse, with a leer
or with eyes to the ground, without a word?
With a sneer, with poisonous laughter,
with a swearword, with a thought, with a forethought?
How do the snipers from the last war
spend the peacetime?
I disarmed myself, buried the gun in the ground.

Then I hung *Dürer's* hare behind the door,
stuffed, with a small mirror around its neck.
The draught in the house
turned it now to the door, now to the patch,
like a pendant hanging from the rear-view mirror,
and it kept beating itself in the little mirror
believing it was hitting another little hare.
In its dream all people were hares,
and all hares people. They waged wars with my gun
till sunrise, undecided, but with casualties.

One day I found my front door gone,
someone had taken it away with him, to his grave or to the market.
Cracked and crumbled the wall gaped,
no gun, no hare, no past.
What else could I hang on it
but the little purse with the key without a keyhole,

with basil tucked in its bow,
and under it a calendar with no year
with tombstone photos
of us all, neither alive nor kicking.

A POEM FROM *GALÁPAGOS*
Malva Flores

translated by
Jennifer Buentello

MY ARRIVAL

Oh, how futile it is to navigate around the islands
—Álvaro Mutis

1.

It took me ten years to return to Galápagos.

Those lists of light flowing like rivers from the sky barely peek through the main island fog. I barely discover the knots in its calligraphy of fish: long silver scale.

How many
        two
           islands
hours pass, a steep peak.
Then, only fog.

The islands manifest themselves from heaven like an incomplete promise: land spreading like beads of a rosary, extending a small prayer.

They didn't see them like that from the Beagle, that ship where the wise man with the long beard searched for his tortoise. His beard like clouds uselessly crossing over this rusty motor flying through the sky.

On the ground, carrying that large shell, the Indica Testudo nigra, carved long paths into the land, seeking water.

And I, looking for the desert. The sands that, I know, are destroying everything.

The cancer of silence.

2.

Promontory crests. From the air, the island's black wrinkles peek out, craters of tuff. And suddenly the sea appears again: the double line of waves crashing on the beach, the plaza glimmering from above. The biggest market, the tugging of pigs, their constant screeches: outrage before death.

3.

The bare mountains are broken, stingy, with a few huisaches: old, dusty plants. Stunted shrubs "sunburnt and can barely survive, covered by a black basaltic lava flow throughout," Darwin said, observing the islands.

Some trees growing in the middle of nowhere cast a brief shadow. Grays that used to be green, I imagine.

We see the ravaged land from the sky. Close by the trail, I make out clear reflections: a large lake of salt or is it water sparkling there?

4.

Crest of the grebe even with the water. The duck's reflection, inconceivable duck with its duckling striped like a zebra.

The invisible mob passes level to the water.

ARRIBO

Oh el infructuoso navegar alrededor de las islas
—Álvaro Mutis

1.

Diez años me tomó regresar a Galápagos.

Esas listas de luz que son los ríos desde el aire apenas si aparecen entre la niebla de la prima isla. Apenas si descubro los nudos en su caligrafía de pez: larga escama de plata.

Cuántas
        dos
            tres islas
al paso de las horas y el escarpado pico.
Luego, sólo la niebla.

Las islas se despliegan desde el cielo como una promesa incumplida: un rosario de tierra donde extender una plegaria mínima.

No las vieron así desde el Beagle, aquel barco donde viajó buscando su tortuga el sabio de las barbas largas. Barbas como las nubes que inútilmente atraviesa este motor roñoso por el cielo.

A ras de suelo, cargando el gran caparazón, Índica Testudo nigra, trazaba largos caminos en la tierra para encontrar el agua.

Y yo, buscando el desierto. Las arenas que, sé, van destruyendo todo.
El cáncer del silencio.

2.

Las crestas del promontorio. Desde el aire se asoman esas arrugas negras de las islas, los cráteres de toba. Y de pronto aparece: de nuevo el mar: la doble fila de las olas chocando con la playa, la plaza que desde arriba atisbo. El mercado mayor, el jalar de los puercos, su chillar de rutina: escándalo que anticipa la muerte.

3.

En los montes pelones se desgajan, tacaños, unos cuantos huizaches: viejas matas polvosas. Raquíticos arbustos "tostados por el sol y que apenas pueden vivir, cubren en toda su extensión una corriente de lava basáltica negra", comentó Darwin al observar las islas.

Algunos árboles plantados en medio de la nada proyectan una breve sombra. Grises que fueron verdes, imagino.

Desde el aire miramos esa tierra arrasada. Cerca ya de la pista se adivinan unos claros reflejos: un gran lago de sal ¿o es agua lo que brilla ahí?

4.

Cresta de somormujo a ras del agua. El reflejo del pato, inconcebible pato con su cría rayada como cebra.

A ras del agua pasa *el tropel invisible.*

I WAS ONLY ABLE TO RECOGNIZE YOU ONCE
Carl-Christian Elze

translated by
Caroline Wilcox Reul

I was only able to recognize you once
in the woods where I sat one may staring
at a little patch of the forest floor
without an ounce of strength in my legs
up to my ears in fear .. a celebration
at the school of veterinary medicine,
an aortic aneurysm the size of a fist
pulsing at the renal artery
near the abdominal wall
for years till it burst: as if my father
had drowned in his own stomach.
when he came to briefly
he was agitated, once he knew
there's not enough time, he became more still ..

I sat there in the woods
without an ounce of strength
in my legs, weighed down
as if by logs,
an ant trail
the only movement
though not a single glance
of these strong fearless
creatures was for me. but you,

you looked at me
from somewhere
from everywhere at once:
through earth
through tree and air.
I became still .. as still
as a speck
under the weight of a log. —
nothing had broken down.
I was a component
of a stable system ..
I would never
break down, never fall out
of that system ..
the end of my existence
simply an inevitable
from time to time necessary
bow
to the earth
at the microscopic level ..
the ritual act of devotion
—since time began.

NUR EINMAL KONNTE ICH DICH ERKENNEN

in einem wald, auf ein stück waldboden starrend
ohne ein krümelchen kraft in den beinen
hockte ich da, im mai, bis zu den ohren
mit angst abgefüllt .. eine feier
im veterinärmedizinischen institut
eine geplatzte aorta, faustgroß
überdehnt, in höhe der nierenabgänge
in die bauchdecke pulsierend
seit jahren: als wäre mein vater
in seinem eigenen bauch ertrunken.
als er noch einmal zu sich kam
wurde er unruhig, erst als er merkte
es reicht nicht allmählich ruhiger ..

ich hockte im wald
ohne ein krümelchen kraft
in den beinen, niedergedrückt
wie von stämmen. —
nur eine ameisenstraße
war noch in betrieb.
aber kein einziger blick dieser
kräftigen, völlig angstfreien
tiere für mich. aber du

du schautest mich an
von irgendwoher
von allen seiten zugleich:
durch erde hindurch
durch bäume und luft.
ich wurde ruhig .. so ruhig
wie eine winzige kugel
unter der last eines stammes. —
nichts brach zusammen.
ich war bestandteil
eines stabilen systems ..
ich würde niemals zusammenbrechen
niemals herausfallen können
aus diesem system ..
das ende meiner existenz
nur eine notwendige
von zeit zu zeit erforderliche
verbeugung
vor der erde
im mikroskopischen bereich ..
das ritual einer liebeserklärung
—seit anbeginn.

TWO POEMS
Liana Sakelliou

translated by
Don Schofield

RAFFAELLO CECCOLI'S ICON, 1853

My father liked the icon
in the monastery because Ceccoli
portrayed his dead daughter as the Virgin.
I was alive and he
was not a painter.
"Only this lasts," he used to whisper
as he held me tightly in his arms
like Ceccoli must have held his heavy easel.

But where was the fountain?
In the lion's mouth?
In the courtyard, beyond the tombs?
Deep in the plane trees' shadows?
I wanted that life-giving spring in the open
so his palm with the unbroken lifeline
would always be there behind the painting.

"Η Ζωοδόχος Πηγή" του Ραφαήλ Τσέκολι, 1853

Στον πατέρα μου άρεσε η εικόνα
στο Μοναστήρι μα πιο πολύ γιατί ο Τσέκολι
ζωγράφισε σαν Παναγία την πεθαμένη κόρη του.
Ήμουν ζωντανή κι εκείνος
δεν ήταν ζωγράφος.
Μόνο αυτή διαρκεί, μου ψιθύριζε.
Με κρατούσε στην αγκαλιά του σφιχτά
όπως ο Τσέκολι το βαρύ καβαλέτο.

Διακρίνεις την κρυμμένη πηγή;
Μέσα στο στόμα του λιονταριού;
Στο προαύλιο, δίπλα στους τάφους;
Βαθειά στα σκιερά πλατάνια;
Διάλεξα την πηγή
Ήθελα την ζωοδόχο πηγή υπαίθρια
αφού η παλάμη του με την ατάραχη γραμμή της ζωής
θα κρυβόταν πάντα πίσω απ' τον πίνακα.

STRETCHER

I was by the sea
searching for the ancient harbor.
Was it sunk by an earthquake?
Plundered by Alaric
and his Visigoths?
I was searching for the epic
of the ancient poets
who left too soon and so were lost.
The cove was small.
A boat was approaching
and the sea was being torn asunder.

ITH

Ήμουν στη θάλασσα.
Έψαχνα το αρχαίο λιμάνι.
Το καταπόντισε ο σεισμός;
Ο Αλάριχος;
Οι Βησιγότθοι;
Έψαχνα τη λέξη των αρχαίων αφηγητών
πως ότι φεύγει, χάνεται.

Ήταν μικρός ο όρμος
το πλοίο όμως πλησίαζε
κι η θάλασσα σκιζόταν.

THROUGH THE MOORS, THROUGH DACHAU
Michaela Maria Müller

translated by
Joe Paul Kroll

I'm back at home. The bread is thawing beside the stove. I pick up the loaf and press it against the blade of the bread slicer. The machine groans, then packs up completely. No chance of cutting a slice off the half-thawed lump of bread. I put the loaf back by the stove. Soon, the house is going to be pulled down. I walk up to the attic.

The smell is of freshly washed laundry. It hangs from lengths of twine and plastic washing line that have been tied together and strung across the room. It's boil wash, a load of udder rags. Worn-out towels, cut into rectangles, hanging side by side from the washing line. They are used to wipe the cows' udders when milking in the morning and in the evening.

Wasps have made their nests under the eaves, sinister grey ovals which they have used their secretions to stick to the beams and the bricks. But the wasps have fallen silent, their nests lie abandoned.

In a drawer, I find a broken pocket-watch, a handful of carnival medals, coins forgotten in coat pockets. The attic has always been full things for which every-day life holds no place.

I pass a hand over the dark wood of the cabinet. Its doors are made of etched glass, and the ends of its side panels turned to form slender columns. It used to belong to a man who had to flee the Nazis, says my grandmother. If her information is correct, it must have been standing here for nearly eighty years.

In the town archives, I find a list of Dachau's Jewish inhabitants. Thirteen names are recorded on the page. The first is that of Samson Gutmann, a livestock dealer. He moves first to Munich, then to Dachau. Rents a house in our neighbourhood, in Freisinger Strasse. The livestock dealer from Dachau and my great-grandfather Michael Müller, a farmer from the next village—did they know each other?

■ ■ ■

When all the children were born, the great-grandparents called for a photographer. It was not long since the last rain. The peaty soil outside the front door was sodden. When the family assembled for the photograph, the soles of their shoes left traces in the earth. The adults sat; the six children stood. Three girls and three boys: Michael, Maria, Josef, Johann, Anna and Lene.

The great-grandfather was wearing a three-piece suit and a freshly starched white shirt. Hair combed severely to one side, the dark moustache waxed. He gazed into the camera, concentrated, his hands clenched into fists above his thighs. My great-grandmother Maria was dressed in a long black frock and wore a watch on a chain around her neck. A small flourish of white frills was visible on each wrist.

They lived by the moor. Its surface was overgrown with low shrubs. The wind gently ruffled the leaves of a rare variety of birch, *Betula humilis*, its seeds washed up here in the last ice age. Its dead wood, along with the twigs and needles of the firs, gradually decomposed to peat. Year by year, century by century, and millimetre by millimetre the ground levelled out, adding a metre in a thousand years.

The moor began at their front door. Anyone coming into the house after the rain brought it inside on the soles of their boots.

The men who worked in the moors were tired when they returned from the day's labours. Cutting peat, they heaved the shiny black bricks full of water out of trenches that led downwards step by step. The deeper, the lower they cut, the denser the peat became. They lifted the wet bricks out of the trenches, inspected and divided them, loaded them onto carts and stacked them to dry in the shacks.

My great-grandmother had packed bread, beer, salted white radish, and cold potatoes for them. The shacks before which they took their repast were knocked together from planks of spruce and open on one side, the better to capture light and warmth and help the peat dry faster.

During these lunch breaks, the older peat cutters taught the younger ones the names of the birds of the moors. Lapwing, barn owl, curlew, snipe. In the late afternoon, they pushed their peat carts homewards.

Once they were ready for burning, my great-grandfather sold the peat bricks to a brewery in Munich, which used them to heat its copper kettles. Back at home, they were used to fire the oven, too. When, of an evening, he watched the peat burning up in the oven, it occurred to him that he was burning the earth that was meant to work for him and his family.

Sometimes the tiredness would linger in the peat cutters' limbs till the next morning and not leave then. The malaria bug had inoculated them with it.

The *Anopheles* mosquito and its brood had reached the ports of the German Empire in overseas cargoes. Thousands of dock workers in the newly-built port of Wilhelmshaven were the first to fall ill. The physician Carl Wenzel reports 4,119 cases among women and children from the Jade Bight alone. The miners of Gelsenkirchen were struck down a little later. The last were the peat-cutting peasant families in the kingdom of Bavaria.

The doctors prescribed quinine. It helped and healed and remained in their medicine cabinets. Since it cured their agues, they made it their cure-all, albeit a pricy one. The crystalline white powder was used as a medicine for other afflictions. It reduced fever and relieved pain. And the maids knew that a large enough dose – ten or twelve grains – would end a pregnancy if taken early on.

In buying the farm, the family had acquired the right to fish the river. The 1863 map shows the river by the name of *Maisach*. They called it by a different name: *Moasa*, its gender female, *die Moasa*.

It is thirty-six kilometres long. In its lower reaches, close to the farm, it comes nearly to a halt, describing ribbons and branching through the swamp like so many little veins on the face of the leas. It takes its time before giving up its name and flowing into a larger river, the Amper.

The graylings, barbels, and breams can grow fifteen years old and taste of the countryside: of the fens.

■ ■ ■

Now the moor has been drained. At the end of the fields, the railway embankment rises. In the daytime, a high-speed train passes every half hour, a local one every quarter, and a commuter train every five minutes. At night, freight trains take over.

By the roadside, a field of gladioli. Cut your own flowers. Fifty metres squared of a meadow just before the sign announces you are entering the town, where the path to the shooting range branches off. The ground close to the beds looks trampled. At the field's age stands an oil drum, painted yellow.

It has been filled with concrete, out of which juts a square metal rod. A laminated price list is attached to this:

Gladioli 70 cents each

Knives dangle from the honesty box, attached by string to a nail. Their blades point downwards.

A firm green stem grows out of the earth, unfolding into leaves higher up. The leaves' veins run in parallel, and the petals are still half rolled up. This one is going to flower in crimson.

I cut plant upon plant. Soon they are more than I can hold in one hand. I stick the knife in the ground and strip off the leaves to reduce the plants' diameter. I leave them lying in the furrows, count out a handful of change and a five-euro note, which I have to fold twice, and put them in the box. In an interview with the local paper, the farmer says that sometimes children try to fish out the paper money with sticky tape, that's why the slit is so narrow.

I drive on eastwards. The gladioli are lying on the back seat. The road used to end at the mill. Heading into town, the walls of the camp are to the right. The local bus is going the other way. Its destination sign reads "744 Kräutergarten."

A bus has been going that way since November 1937. It was district commissioner Böhmer who, in late July, had applied to the regional government of Upper Bavaria for a new bus route to be set up.

The district commissioner asks the Dachau cab drivers for an estimate of how often they had driven the route between the station, the camp, and the town over the past six months.

Over two thousand times is the figure he gives in his application. A thousand errands to run. Visiting the cobbler, going for treatment at Doktor Blank's spa, seeing Herr Meisinger at the health board or Herr Köhler at the bank, appointments with Headmaster Götz or Doktor Franta the vet, purchases at Wülfert's sausage factory or Herr Siems the tobacconist's. The line is opened for service before his application has even been granted.

Henceforth two buses ply the route between the station and the camp: two omnibuses made by Daimler-Benz, straight from the factory, their engines stamped with consecutive serial numbers, registered B-52230 and B-52227, with thirty-two seats apiece.

A year later the moor became the *Kräutergarten*, the herb garden. Inmates had to dig kilometre-long drainage ditches, dig up the earth, pile on fertile soil, parcel out beds, plant shrubs and gladioli bulbs.

In late summer, they cut the plants and squeezed the juice from the leaves. It was used to produce synthetic vitamin C, ascorbic acid.

The extract was mixed to a paste with thyme, lovage, salt, and beef fat, and sent to the front as the base for a fortifying drink in individually wrapped portions.

■ ■ ■

This April, persistent ground frost means that the municipal gardeners are behind in their work. The trees that are to be planted lie side by side on the lawn. Each root ball is wrapped in several layers of sacking, the cloth tied around the trunk.

I meet an amateur beekeeper who tells me about his hives. This April is so cold, he says, that the bees can't leave the hive. They eat the honey themselves. He gives a regretful shrug.

The glass of the Kräutergarten greenhouses is broken. Rust has eaten deep into the iron braces. Grass is beginning to grow over the borders of the plant beds. Over the decades, the weather has shifted the concrete parts, which jut out the lawn at peculiar angles. Green moss and yellow lichen have spread over them.

After the war, the administrative buildings were converted into flats.

Now, yellow paint is peeling off the walls. In places where holes were drilled, the plaster chips off in pieces the size of a hand, the mortar crumbles to the ground in a dry trickle. The letter-boxes are marked with Arab names in Latin script. Someone has stuck a notice reading "Please no advertisement" on their box. In a crack between the street and the building's foundations, dandelion flourishes alongside herb robert.

I feel somebody watching me. A woman is looking out of a first-floor window. When our glances meet, she avoids mine and fixes hers on the still-empty beds belonging to the council.

Old apple trees stand in front of the buildings. The municipal gardeners have attached signs to the trunks:

Cultivar
'Rhenish Winter Rambo'
Ready to eat: December to March
Flavour: mildly sweet and tart
Chance seedling – ancient variety – c. 1650
Dachau Town Council
Department of Municipal Greenery and the Environment

The residents have placed a white plastic table and a folding wooden bench under one of the chestnut trees. Two wooden chairs are attached to each other by a combination lock, as though it was a promise.

A man steps out of the door to collect his mail from the box. A woman joins him, they start talking about a phone bill. I ask them if they know something about the buildings' past. They shake their heads. "No, no idea," they say.

The woman points towards the playground across the road, which belongs to a new housing development, and says: "But look, that one's new."

She thinks I'm asking because the buildings are in such poor repair, though what I mean is their past. I understand that these aspects belong together.

■ ■ ■

My grandfather is in a "scheduled occupation," as they call it. He is thirty-one years old. He does not yet have a family of his own. He is stuck between the threat of being called up for service in the war and his duties tending to the farm.

One day before Christmas, 1940, he takes a bound volume from the drawer in the kitchen table. The leatherette cover is labelled "Accounts of the Mittern-dorf-Udlding Commons." He enters the following:

Maisach de-iced, ½ day, 2 marks

The village works the wood in common. Twenty-two farmers, a blacksmith, a master saddler, a master joiner, and a locksmith, as well as their families.

Grandfather is the head. Each family has two facing pages to itself, and each job is tallied according to a fixed rate. Thin red lines separate the columns.

Firewood in the shed and lumber for the new stables are a liability, work done in the woods an asset. Two members don't go into the woods, their asset page left blank: the owner of the paper factory and the priest.

Six weeks later, at the end of January 1941, supplies of firewood are exhausted. Grandfather, together with the other men who are not at the front, spends three days in the wood. He notes:

Work in the wood, manual and carriage tasks, 3 days, 23 marks

May is when the annual wood auction is held, where firewood and planks of lumber may be won. Afterwards, everybody goes to the tavern together.

The bar tab can still be found in the old accounts book, to which it is attached by a rusty paper-clip:

```
30 pints lager:        9.—
3 pints white beer:    1.14
Sausages:              4.70
15 B.Pol:             −.75
                    _____
                      15.59
                       1.55
                    _____
                      17.14
```

Two years later, grandfather is called up, first to the barracks at Kempten, later to Landsberg-on-Lech for driver training, then to the front as a dispatch driver. When his father dies on Christmas Day, 1944, he receives home leave. He buries his father, marries, and sees his two-month-old son. He will have to hope a long time for a reunion. Only five years later will he return.

■ ■ ■

I am sitting in the archives and running my index finger over an old map of the town, find the station and, alongside it, Adolf-Hitler-Strasse. Why did they choose that one? The street is not particularly long, perhaps six hundred metres or so, and begins to the right of the station parade. I trace the street to its end.

Yet then there are the four grid squares that are the site of twelve years of murder and suffering. They are left blank. No barracks are marked, no industrial wasteland, residential areas, fenland, or woods. The railway track by which inmates were transported to the camp ends in the middle of nowhere.

The town map informs me that at the end of the track are to be found the South German Reed Mat Works and a power station, the "Amperwerke."

"Why?" I ask the archivist. "Restricted area. Military," he replies.

The huge void on the map shows no sign of getting smaller.

I meet somebody who knows more. Kurt is waiting for me at the entrance to the former SS training camp. Now, the grounds are a training facility for the Bavarian riot police. The guards, two young police officers, wave us through. It all goes quickly, so quickly that I'm surprised. No ID check, not even eye contact.

"We're expected," he says when he registers my surprise. He trained Bavarian riot police for forty years. Maybe he was their instructor.

Kurt is wearing a backpack and pushing a bicycle. He offers me the use of a bicycle parked alongside the gatehouse.

The pedal bearings crack as I ride it. On each turn of the pedals, my left leg seems to tread into empty space for half a rotation. I double the force in my left leg to keep up with him.

"What was it like to work here?" I ask.

"I spent a long time trying to find out who used to work in my office. But they destroyed most of the files. I never did find out," he says.

We stop at a bridge overgrown with moss. A weatherworn stone tablet bears the inscription "Samoa Bridge." Whoever gave it that name dreamed of paradise as a colonial empire in the South Pacific.

From his backpack, Kurt takes a blue ring binder and opens it. He shows me our route on an old map. This time, the map is not one with empty grid squares, not this one. They neatly recorded each building. Where we are now standing, the map shows a railway track branching off to the right and ending at three black squares.

"What's that?" I ask.

"Ammo bunker," he says.

During the First World War, officials in the Bavarian war ministry decided to build a new gunpowder and ammunition factory.

There already was such a factory in Ebenhausen, sixty kilometres away. The officials had seven sites to choose from. They decided on Dachau, because the town and its environs were located in an area that was rich in water but had a low incidence of thunderstorms.

Hundreds of workshops, houses, and facilities were rapidly built and populated with workers virtually overnight. The town's population doubled within a year. The workers lived in hastily erected shacks and were soon followed by their families. The classrooms thronged with school children.

We dismount outside a Portakabin and sit down on a bench. During the week, police cadets live here. There is no-one to be seen on a Sunday afternoon.

We are now quite close to the water tower from the days of the munitions factory, and to the memorial next door, too. A wire fence surrounds the water tower, it's cordoned off, no entry. The same applies at the next stop. A construction fence blocks access to the "Holländerhalle," named after the machines used to make guncotton.

"Controlled deterioration," remarks Kurt.

The Holländerhalle is a tall, airy building in which the women's hands would receive acid burns as they worked. Their hands turned yellow. Behind their backs, the townspeople would call the women canaries.

We take a shortcut across a patch of grass to the entrance of a long, single-story building, covered in grey plaster and roofed with brown tiles. Three cars are parked in front of it. Kurt gets off his bicycle. I stop alongside him. A strong wind has picked up. I try to rub sand from my right eye, it tears up, I want to press on. He stops me, says: "The Dachau trials were held in there."

We can't enter, it's locked.

■ ■ ■

On my next visit home, fresh gravel has just been spread in the yard. Where the house stood, beds of leeks, beans, parsley have been planted. Hollyhocks and zinnias grow in between. For years it rained through the roof, there was no saving the house. Its substance was too badly damaged, the materials used had been of poor quality.

At an angle of forty-five degrees to the right of where the house had once stood, builders have excavated a pit. Behind it the pen for the Simmental cattle, which was so modern in the early 1980s that delegations from Japan would come to visit it. They paid to have their pictures taken with us children in coins which they had strung through holes on a cord.

The cabinet from the attic is now in my aunt's flat. I am unable to trace Samson Gutmann's descendants. Did he escape and survive? Was his entire family murdered? Why is name not in the central database of Holocaust victims at the Yad Vashem memorial in Israel? There is a story to all of Dachau's other Jewish citizens. Children who were sent to England, parents who perished in concentration camps in the East. Adults who returned in memory of their childhood ending.

WITHOUT A PLACE
Yente Serdatsky

translated by
Cady Vishniac

Translator's Note: *It's easy to interpret this story of family abandonment as a thinly veiled account of Yente Serdatsky's own abandonment (and later reconciliation) with her husband and children. What a reader might miss is that it's also about the effect of modernity on Eastern European Jews, or Ashkenazim. The protagonist is frustrated by family life in part because of the breakdown of industrialization's impact on the economic systems that once supported the Ashkenazim—her husband earns very little and they have several children, likely with more to come. She is also frustrated because she's been exposed to new leftist politics popular among educated Jews of her time, only to have many benefits of modernity denied to her as a woman. She struggles with familial love; she is conscious that her position in the family is unfair.*

In this story we understand that internal struggle that so many Jewish women felt, the pull between family as a source of comfort and family as a burden imposed by her class, culture, and time, made more of a burden by destitution.

Everything turned out as Mirl wanted. She'd been in the great, busy city of V—— for some months. She had to fight a whole war in order to attain this; finally, she emerged the victor.

Eight years back Mirl got married. At the time she was eighteen years old. She didn't have any real concept of marriage; she only sensed that some unfamiliar feelings were forming in her, that it was somewhat too crowded in her parents' house, and that she must begin a new life . . . or so she thought. That after the wedding she would pass a boundary to some sort of new, bright life—no other path had she imagined at the time. And she hadn't fooled herself: their small room on the third floor, which she and her Shmuel moved into after the wedding, was always full of people, and these people brought with them a world of new ideas. In her little apartment rang out young, energetic voices, which valiantly constructed this new world, a free world.

Mirl began to mature: many things that had earlier lain hidden deep in her soul, expressed only as an inconceivable longing, became clear to her. So passed three years, and on the day when Mirl's path became clear to her, she was already fenced in with four children; children don't want to know their mother's plans, and require their own. Her Shmuel didn't earn much, and she had to look after the home, cook, sew, and do the washing.

The day would pass in constant busywork. One day went after the other, one week after the other, and Mirl had lost her patience. She would then think, "Will my whole youth pass this way?"

At this thought she would tremble with fear. She would try to stop thinking of herself. She would try to get used to it—to see her happiness, her future, only in the children.

That's when the war began for her, a hard, bitter war. She was twenty-one years old, full of strength and life. In her soul coursed desire and ambition, immensely drawn into the great world. She *had to* start a new life, a life that was meaningful to her, and her only thought was to tear herself from home, from her children and husband. For six years she'd wanted this. She'd lost so many forces in the war. Both her body and soul suffered for it; she perceived this all too well, but she nevertheless tore herself away.

Now she's lived several months in the tumultuous city. She's registered for and begun to attend courses. She's prepared herself to lead the new life of which she dreamed for so long. In the meantime, she still can't settle on a room.

The first room she rents from an old woman, a widow. Right away on the very first night, when Mirl sits herself down by the little old woman on the balcony, the old woman suddenly begins to speak of *him*, may he rest in peace, what a kind-hearted person he was, and of her beautiful, gifted children, who are spread across the whole world. Mirl sits the whole time as if nailed to the spot and listens deeply: she sees how the little old woman's dull eyes, speaking of her children, flare up, and her wrinkled face becomes almost smooth.

Suddenly, Mirl's mind is confused by strange thoughts. "This woman has lived three generations," thinks Mirl, "and yet is still sustained by her family life, just as she was when she was young."

The whole time, Mirl takes to leafing through her own marriage. She can't remember one good thing, nothing at all similar to what she hears from the old woman. The first three years, Mirl lived in a tumult, and the last five, it seemed, she hated both her Shmuel and the children. She saw in them only the fence that stood between her and life, and this was enough to make her hate them. They, it seemed to her, had paid her back in kind—it couldn't, of course, be otherwise. And she sees herself in the future, an old woman, stooped exactly like her current landlady, but without the warm family memories. A lonesome woman, despondent.

She puts her hand over her forehead and gets up from her place—stupid thoughts—and tries to drive away her melancholy.

The other evenings pass the same. The old lady comes to further confide in her, and Mirl deserts the room and looks for a new landlady.

In the new apartment, however, lives a family with two children, and Mirl often imagines that the children are strangely similar to her own. Here, it seems to her, is her little Chaim, with his blond, curly hair, with his deep blue, thoughtful eyes, and with rosy little cheeks; and there, the younger has exactly the same dark grey eyes as her little Laybl. Even the voice is like Laybl's. Not intentionally, Mirl takes to looking at the mother. She sees how happy the mother is, like she's delighted by each word from the children. It seems that with each look at the children, the mother is rejuvenated.

More than anything, Mirl suffers in the morning, when they dress their children. The mother looks and beams at, beams and kisses the dressed-up little children, and the children scramble all the while, one with little arms around the mother's neck, covering it with kisses.

Mirl is reminded that each time she dressed her children, they used to become nervous and upset. "Nonsense," she would think with anger. When would she be done with this "nonsense"!

And she would comb their hair with anger, dress them with anger, and go away from them with anger. The children used to stand the whole time with lowered heads, like sinners, and used to breathe a sigh of relief as soon as she left.

Mirl feels a twinge of remorse; something seethes in her heart. Now she wants to dress her children with love, like the young mother, and to take them in her arms and kiss them. How good that would be—weakness, softness. She frets, and without staving off further weakness, she rents another room.

Now she has, it seems, truly arrived. Middle-aged people, grown children, all good. Time to go study. She tells herself, "This behind on my studies, who knows whether I will catch up?"

And she's tried to take to the books. Only, right across from her lives a young couple in love. Whole days, one after another, they kiss each other. The textbook falls from Mirl's hand, for suddenly, before her eyes, her Shmuel appears. She sees his high white forehead with its beautiful widow's peak, with its soft, blue, gentle eyes, which used to always look at her with such love—before she left she saw such pleading in his eyes—and now it seems to her she senses his warm breath, and she recalls with what hate she used to ward him off. She doesn't know why she hated him so much, only that he stood in her path, and that was enough that she drove him away.

Mirl feels an urgent longing to have her Shmuel near her. Now, she'd take his head in both hands and look him long, long in his blue, gentle eyes. He would, it seems to her, die of joy. And she?

Only enough! Enough. To Mirl, the thought is simply shameful.

She has to get away from this apartment.

She has rented a room from an old maid. "Here, finally nothing will be in my way," she thinks, and begins to set out her things.

Only. Only soon, she senses the apartment is ruled over by a deep, sad stillness, a stillness like in a cemetery. She can't bear the old maid's look; she feels such melancholy, sorrow, and longing in the look that it tugs at her heart. The old maid's eyes speak to her of a long history, of an eternally lonesome life, of unhappiness and eternal longing. Mirl feels crowded there. She can't breathe the air there, and she's suffocating . . . and looks for a new apartment.

Her books lie unopened.

And she can't keep any fixed address.

BOOK REVIEWS

The Secret of Black Girl Magic:
MEET BEHIND MARS
Renee Simms

and

WHAT IT MEANS WHEN A MAN FALLS FROM THE SKY
Lesley Nneka Arimah

reviewed by

Rochelle Spencer

Meet Behind Mars
Stories by Renee Simms
Wayne State University Press, May 2018
$18.99, 144 pp.
ISBN-13: 978-0814345122

What It Means When a Man Falls from the Sky
Stories by Lesley Nneka Arimah
Riverhead Books, April 2017
$26.00, 240 pp.
ISBN-13: 978-0735211025

> I should be clear: Black women are not superheroes. We hurt and bleed and are vulnerable and tired . . . But our ability to defy, persist, and excel in the face of systematic oppression is a magical beast . . .
> —Idrissa Simmonds, from *The BreakBeat Poets, Vol. 2: Black Girl Magic*. Ed. Mahogany L. Browne, Idrissa Simmonds, and Jamila Woods

Freedom. This idea is infused in two recent short story collections that address the question, in situations where you're tied to a job or to a partner by economic or familial ties, how do you escape?

Renee Simms's *Meet Behind Mars* (Wayne State University Press, 2018) and Lesley Nneka Arimah's *What It Means When A Man Falls From the Sky* (Riverhead Books, 2017) contemplate escape. In these stories magic burns at the center, or at least, warms and singes the edges. But these stories are magical not because of fantastical elements but because of their investigation of how and why people try to escape. Simms and Arimah cast spells with imperfect women battling society's many trolls and demons, including its hierarchical authorities and structures. These women don't always do what society expects of them, and that's the point. Through these stories, we better understand liberation: preserving who you are and finding ways to defy, challenge, or resist.

In the first story in Simms's collection, "High County," the protagonist, Hathoria, or Hattie, wants to be a writer. She sometimes resents being a wife and mother and the steady plod of ordinary life (Hattie's mother-in-law lives in a retirement community where "the squat tan and olive houses look like tortoises lined up close together"). A strange and brilliant moment occurs when Hattie meets characters from stories she's read:

> "They're gone," Arleta says. "Isn't that what you wanted, sugar? For them to be gone so that you could write?" Hattie stares at Arleta. She is aware of the heat again and of the sweating that she can't control. A ceiling fan whirls above, moving the dusty air around. Arleta takes a swig of her beer, then lets out a loving belch. "I've been waiting for you to write me into one of your stories," she says. "Look—my hair turned white I've been waiting so long."

These characters offer to "loan" themselves to Hattie, so that she can finish her novel. Hattie's interactions with these characters matter; they offer proof that Hattie's writing is her best strategy for asserting her autonomy. Hattie realizes this herself: "If she can find the strength, her story is on the verge of breaking open and revealing the world exactly as she sees it."

Simms reveals the strange in the mundane. In "Dive," Alex, visiting her adoptive parents, describes the creepiness of the suburbs: "There's a reason why so many horror movies have had suburban settings. I dare you to look out at night at the expanse of an unlit backyard and not see eyes lurking in the hedge." But even though the world can sometimes seem unsetting and mysterious, Alex understands how life's repetition, "those moments when the past and present converged and time felt like a loop," can leave us feeling trapped, as we try to carve out our own spaces and are forced, sometimes, to create space for family and responsibility, "to make room, somehow, for a grown man and a baby." And the flood of emails from Gloria Clark, the mother in "Meet Behind Mars," beautifully illustrates how raising a black child in a hostile and punishing society can be exhausting.

Set in Detroit, the Motor City, perhaps Simms's fiction can't help but explore ideas of freedom and movement. "American Industrial Physics" manages to allude to both the automobile industry and to the animal rights activism questions explored in Kaitlyn Greenidge's *We Love You, Charlie Freedman*. Greenidge and Simms explore how black women's intellectual work can serve as refuge— one's curiosity and imagination can offer (some) fulfillment even when society oppresses. Simms's Dr. Johnetta Green, who cares for the test monkeys at Ford Motor Company, may question the importance of motherhood and nurturing more than Greenidge's Laurel Freeman, the black woman scientist who teaches a monkey sign language. Simms, like Greenidge, explores the parameters of compassion: how much should we nurture our children, what responsibilities do we have towards ourselves?

Arimah similarly constructs fiction with fantastical moments and realistic stories with elements of wonder and escape. "Wild" and "War Stories" are stories about why we tell stories, how we try to escape by requesting someone else witness our pain. In "Wild," two warring cousins acknowledge their secrets and grow close, even as sexism limits their freedom. In "War Stories," a family shares stories that reveal how, in the process of telling a story, we generate not only empathy but also resilience, the ability to navigate "the strangeness . . . the growing moroseness" saturating our lives. In "Wild" and "War Stories" we once again see rebellious girls, almost women, not afraid to be themselves. The magic in these two more realistic stories can be found in how much Arimah celebrates—or at least acknowledges—that rebellion. When Nwando, the girl protagonist of "War Stories," is criticized by her mother for harassing her classmates, Nwando is unapologetic. Ada, the teenaged protagonist of "Wild," witnesses her mother high on ecstasy (because Ada has disguised ecstasy pills in an Excedrin bottle) and doesn't exactly feel shame for her behavior. "Light" reveals Arimah's commitment to female protagonists who enjoy breaking the rules. At the end of "Light," a father mourns the independent-minded daughter who becomes meek and loses her "streak of fire." "Redemption," the story that closes the collection, describes how Mayowa, a young female servant, mischievously challenges the mistreatment directed at poor young women.

There's magic in seeing complicated girls and women argue, rebel, and attempt to live as they want. Yet when Arimah ventures into magic and fantasy, her protagonists' realities stun. The pain cuts sharp when a young woman sees her dead mother in "Second Chances." Nnwam feels guilty about her mother's death, and this story, about what we'd say to our loved ones if given the opportunity, haunts us. "Who Will Greet You at Home" and the collection's eponymously titled story Afrofuturist story are breathtaking. Both rely on folklore adeptly embedded into the narrative (Otesánek, the Flying Africans). Hope and survival steady these fable-esque stories with a keen emotional realism. "Who Will Greet You at Home" transports us into a world where poor women create living babies out of the materials around them (yarn, grass, mud, hair), with the hope that their children can live better lives.

"What It Means When a Man Falls from the Sky" explores the complexities of empathy. Nneoma is a prickly contrarian. Even though she comprehends a mathematical formula for reducing human suffering, she decides to use that information to help only a few. Nnemoa is a study in self-preservation; what seems like selfishness may be armor against how caretakers, in many cases women, are unfairly burdened with emotional labor. Even though the story contains fantastic elements, its pessimism seems realistic, warranted. But I wonder if more time could be spent exploring the pleasure in forming human connections.

Traditionally, in black culture, the conjure woman had more power than other people in her community. By showing complex, contemporary women who encounter magic and occasionally wield it, Simms and Arimah allow us to understand the radiance of everyday life. The phrase "Black Girl Magic" is originated by a black woman, Cashawn Thompson. Maybe in the era of #blacklivesmatter, a movement founded by black women—Alicia Garza, Patrisse Cullors, and Opal Tometi—and the Tarana Burke-led #metoo movement, we're discovering what it means to be truly magical.

TRANS*: A QUICK AND QUIRKY
ACCOUNT OF GENDER VARIABILITY
Jack Halberstam

reviewed by

Rhonda Lancaster

Trans*: A Quick and Quirky Account of Gender Variability
Nonfiction by Jack Halberstam
University of California Press, January 2018
$18.95; 184 pp.
ISBN-13: 978-0520292697

Trans*: A Quick and Quirky Account of Gender Variability by Jack Halberstam
lives up to the first part of its subtitle. At a slim 138 pages of content, it gives a
quick overview of a very complex issue. Calling it "quirky" might be debatable
though. Halberstam has written a straightforward thesis about "gender vari-
ance," but the use of pop culture to frame the argument is an unusual step for
an academic text. Overall, the book offers a unique voice in the discourse. Hal-
berstam addresses two specific aspects of trans* theories: nomenclature as both
liberating and limiting and the physical representation of bodies.

As Halberstam explains in the first chapter, he chose trans* with the asterisk
to "open the term up to unfolding categories of being organized around but
not confined to forms of gender variance." He continues explaining that the
asterisk "modifies the meaning of transitivity by refusing to situate transition
in relation to a destination, a final form, a specific shape, or an established con-
figuration of desire and identity." The use of the asterisk is not unique to Jack,
but using it adds to the philosophy he hopes his audience will accept: that our
world needs more options for gender than the current accepted labels.

While Halberstam acknowledges his own experience with top surgery and
his feelings of not fitting the body to which he was born, this is not a mem-

oir. He only briefly mentions his own experience near the beginning, when acknowledging that *Trans** may address the more masculine perspective because of his experience, and during the chapter on trans* feminism. It is vital that this personal experience is addressed when discussing feminism since there is still a strain between some feminists who view transsexuals as "interlopers into spaces that women had fought hard to protect from men" and feminists who see no such distinction. Jack encourages society to acknowledge sexism, misogyny, and transphobic "chatter" in its multiple forms by sharing several personal reflections.

The book begins by tracing the historical legacies of categorization and classification as they pertain to the transgender body, moves through the historical and current use of augmentative surgeries, the experience of being trans or parenting a trans* child, and trans* representations in film and on TV, and finally, discusses trans* feminism, a contentious subject. Throughout, Halberstam uses pop culture references from the opening David Bowie epitaph ("You've got your mother in a whirl/She's not sure if you're a boy or a girl") to the closing dissection of what *The Lego Movie* (2014) says "about building new worlds, new architectures, and trans* relations to bodies and selves." In between, he references *Game of Thrones* and *Finding Nemo* (2003). All this is outside the chapter on trans* representations in film, which analyzes the mainstream films, *The Crying Game* (1992) and *Boys Don't Cry* (1999), and lesser known *By Hook or By Crook* (2001) and indie film *The Aggressives* (2005). This chapter wouldn't be complete without a discussion of *Transparent* as a television series that successfully represents a "specific trans experience . . . without making it representative of *all* trans experience" (*italics* the author's).

In Chapter 2, "Making Trans* Bodies," Halberstam makes the argument that transgenderism needs to be placed within a new biopolitical regime where "bodies are not simply the effect of performative or social constructions." He describes not only the changing terminology of sexual and gender diversity, but the more widespread emphasis on defying the classification, the established norms, and identities. He discusses the step away from psychological or physiological notions to that of pharmaceutical enhancement (Viagra, contraception, hormones, etc.). This leads into a discussion of health concerns not currently addressed, such as male balding for transmen or waning libido for transwomen. He expands writer Maggie Nelson's comparison of her pregnancy to her partner's experiences with top surgery. Nelson writes, "bearing each other loose witness," and Halberstam adds this "captures not just the experience of partnering with a trans* person but the experience of partnering in general."

Nowhere is Halberstam as concise as in the final chapter, "Conclusions," wherein he creates an analogy of *The Lego Movie* with his vision "where the future is not male or female but transgender." He describes Lego architecture as a constant state of emergence and collapse as children assemble, knock down, and rebuild environments. In the movie, the humanoid characters seek a fabled "piece of resistance" that is "part phallus, part vessel" and literal cap to the superglue weapon the antagonist Lord Business plans to use to prevent the continual transition of the world around him. Halberstam compares Lord Business to the portion of the world who would like to fix gender into the neat division of two categories and the "piece of resistance" to the force of trans* recreation. He finishes by discussing the current dispute about "bathroom bills" and how solving this single issue will not solve the overarching issue of equality and acceptance. He brings together his arguments on nomenclature and body as he argues that we should not simply look for a solution that grants or denies access, but "rethinks the function, the purpose, and the productive force of the architectures we inhabit." He closes by encouraging us to see the trans* body as all the negatives that history applied as well as a "site for invention, imagination, fabulous projection."

*Trans** was not the "quirky" and thereby "light" read I was expecting, but it was undeniably educational on a complex issue that is currently under debate in our classrooms, courtrooms, and social interactions. Throughout this review, I've chosen to use "he" as the personal pronoun for the author because of references by the author about favoring masculinity and the use of the male pronoun in promotional blurbs that accompanied the book; however, in an addendum, Jack refuses to answer the question about pronouns saying, "the back and forth between he and she sort of captures the form that my gender takes nowadays." Much as Jack, formerly Judith, Halberstam refuses to choose a gender pronoun, preferring to leave it ambiguous along the lines of transitivity, *Trans** does not provide a definitive answer to what should or must be done. It does, however, add to the discourse on transitivity with an important argument toward an expansion of perspective through our use of nomenclature and our view of embodiment.

COOKING WITH THE MUSE:
A SUMPTUOUS GATHERING OF SEASONAL RECIPES,
CULINARY POETRY, AND LITERARY FARE
Myra Kornfeld and Stephen Massimilla

reviewed by

Susan Thurston

Cooking with the Muse: A Sumptuous Gathering of Seasonal Recipes, Culinary Poetry, and Literary Fare
Recipes and more by Myra Kornfeld and Stephen Massimilla
Tupelo Press, April 2016
$32.95; 500 pp.
ISBN-13: 978-1936797684

Cooking with the Muse: A Sumptuous Gathering of Seasonal Recipes, Culinary Poetry, and Literary Fare is a culinary-reader of delights nested together much like a matryoshka doll. With hundreds of recipes, poetic prose pieces, cooking and poetry notes, and lavish illustrations, this literary cookbook defies simple classification. Authors Myra Kornfeld and Stephen Massimilla offer a lap-filling volume that could be criticized for overreach if it weren't such a fascinating genre-blending, seasonally-framed journey through history and culture.

The dense, luxurious volume begs to be taken from the kitchen to the bedside. Distractions and redirections are tucked into the "Poet's Notes." The note for "Anasazi Bean Chili with Roasted Eggplant" informs that, in Milton's "Paradise Lost," the purpled-colored Apples of Sodom that Lucifer's fallen angels consume are eggplants. Or you'll encounter references to contemporary poems, such as Ellen Bass's "Eating the Bones" in the "Roasted Butterflied Sumac Chicken" recipe.

The recipe introductions are poems themselves, as "Baked Seckel Pears with Pomegranate Syrup" instructs readers to "spoon the hot red juices over [the pears] at regular intervals as they bake, until they are wrinkled and tender as antique Italian wine skins."

The recipe narratives might at first seem over-written, but they possess a seductive elegance. Sophisticated culinary terms, from chiffonade to mirepoix, are made understandable and possible for even the uninitiated cook. Descriptions of ethnic dishes such as colcannon and bastilla become invitations to create. And the measurements are accurate, as all of the recipes tested produced the promised results.

Along with highlights by literary anchors from John Keats to Grace Paley, Kornfeld and Massimilla's own poetry adds flavorful sumptuousness to dozens of the recipes. Many would serve well as an introduction read aloud when presenting a dinner party dish. For example, table guests would thrill to a plattered presentation of "Seared Duck with Plum Sauce," with the cook reciting the paired poems:

> "Plum Hunger"
> Distant honk of train,
> Moon streaked with ducks
> over wine-summer marsh.

with

> "After Basho"
> Never forget to see
> in sockets of the thicket
> night-black eyes of plums.

This book would be welcomed by anyone passionate about history, poetry, and food. The writing alone will have readers feeling plump and blissful with satiating narratives and sensual themes.

Now, it is time for this reviewer to get back into the kitchen to create "Warm-Hearted Pea Cakes with Sesame Crust and Garlic-Piquillo Pepper Sauce," or "Delicata Squash with Cranberry-Date Cornbread Stuffing," or "Salad of a Thousand Leaves."

IRRADIATED CITIES
Mariko Nagai

reviewed by

Katharine Coldiron

Irradiated Cities
Poems by Mariko Nagai
Les Figues Press, August 2017
$17.00, 144 pp.
ISBN-13: 978-1934254684

Irradiated Cities is impossible to leave at a remove from one's own body. It is a discomfiting revelation and a devastating indictment of one of the twentieth century's defining forces: nuclear power. The book is a narrative of cities, not a story told via the standard Aristotelian model, and as such it continually zooms in and out. *In* to the granular details of people's individual lives and sufferings, and *out* to an atrocity that stains an entire nation. *In* to the shape and subject of a historical photograph of a radiation victim, and *out* to an archive that contains tens of thousands of similar photos.

The book offers the stories of four cities: Hiroshima, Nagasaki, Tokyo, and Fukushima. Of these, reasonably well-informed readers might wonder at Tokyo, because no nuclear bomb or accident ever caused in Tokyo the kind of catastrophe the other three cities have undergone. But Nagai uses Tokyo as a point of transition between war-devastated Japan and how, in rebuilding, the nation returned to nuclear devastation of a different kind. From "How to Build Nuclear Power Plants" in the Tokyo section:

: it must be a place that believes in the goodness of the government : *it is for the national prosperity, your sacrifices are small compared to what Japan can be—economically rich* : it must be a place that will believe you when you tell them, *nuclear energy is a clean energy, no one has ever died from nuclear energy* : it must be a place where people are practical because practicality is how they have survived during lean months : it must be a place where when they see deformed fish, they will shrug and keep eating them : it must be a place that when you tell them you will build real roads & hospitals, & better schools, they will look at you (you think) in gratitude for the future now possible :

This fragmented, low-punctuation prose style is how the entire book is written—uncapitalized bits of language divided by spaced colons. The work on these pages feels like neither poetry nor prose and is often more matter-of-fact than it is lyric. But the effect, as the facts and figures of the collection build and build, is overwhelming. The injustices done to these places, and the people who inhabited them, scream in blood and fire, even though the photographs are (mostly) nonviolent, black and white, and sometimes as simple as a shadow or a brick wall.

The language is usually as simple as the photographs, but it's a deceptive simplicity. The pieces build individually, from the top of the page to the bottom, as well as building over the collection. "Twenty-Four Hours," in the Fukushima section, begins:

: it is always beautiful on a catastrophic day : it is beautiful because the *before* is beautiful & the *after* dreadful : it is a beautiful day because it must be :

And the closing of "Before the Before & After the After," in the Nagasaki section, reads:

: each retelling puts rumors closer to truth until truth & hearsay become one & the same :

Certain terms haunt the collection. The Japanese words for the nuclear flash and its following sound, *pika* and *don*; the name for the survivors of either of the twin nuclear blasts in 1945, *hibakusha*. But the true specter of the book is the men who make world-altering decisions, toying with forces greater than they can contain, without considering the human cost. The callous choices leading to these nuclear disasters—whether wartime or peacetime—are impossible to contemplate without rage. Yet this is not an angry book. Implacably, Nagai holds up a mirror to the wretched consequences of these men's choices. One of the pictures is of the blood-drenched coat of a doctor who worked in Nagasaki on August 9, 1945, and it is perhaps the truest picture in the book.

Hence, there is only one piece in the collection that is enjoyably impactful instead of distressingly so: "A Man, Hiroshima, and Bikini Atoll." The pleasure of this piece derives from its subject, a certain monster who has alternately destroyed and protected Tokyo since his birth in 1954, even unto the present day.

: a creature is born : *gojira* : the divine, the destroyer, the avenger, the godlike : it rises from the sea : *Godzilla* :

Even though it's a treat to see him show up in *Irradiated Cities*, Godzilla is not played for laughs in this piece. It's no stretch to envision him as a consequence of the nuclear horrors undergone by Japanese citizens (just as the bomb inspired so many Big Bug movies in America in the 1950s). But in this piece, Nagai points out that Godzilla's creator was directly inspired by his experiences in Hiroshima and of the Bikini Atoll tests. And she notes, through the depth of language and the accelerating rhythm of the piece, that Godzilla is no less important, no less a cultural force, than the bloodier consequences of the war. He just works in a different register than children trapped in hospitals while their flesh rots from the inside out.

Thus, Nagai demonstrates herself capable of working in multiple registers as a writer. Perhaps it's her versatility (she is also the collection's photographer) that makes this collection so extraordinary, or perhaps it's the source material, but the real reason may be the calm way that the atrocities Nagai writes on are presented. In its own way, the book is as convincing as the terrible men who caused its horrors.

LET DEAD GIRLS SPEAK:
THE VIRGINIA STATE COLONY FOR EPILEPTICS AND FEEBLEMINDED
Molly McCully Brown

and

THRUST
Heather Derr-Smith

reviewed by

Gillian Neimark

The Virginia State Colony for Epileptics and Feebleminded
Poems by Molly McCully Brown
Persea Books, March 2017
80 pp., $15.95
ISBN-13: 978-0892554782

Thrust
Poems by Heather Derr-Smith
Persea Books, October 2017
96 pp., $15.95
ISBN-13: 978-0892554867

"A dead girl can kick a movie into gear," writes poet Kim Addonizio, in *what is this thing called love,* "better than a salon brawl, better / than a factory explosion." The most memorable dead girl of post-confessional poetry lies decaying in the woods in Frank Bidart's chilling masterpiece "Herbert White." The narrator—a serial killer, pedophile, and necrophiliac—hits a girl on the head: "it was good / and then I did it to her a couple of times." He deposits her body in the woods after raping her yet is drawn back time and again. He even jumps out of the car, leaving his family for a few minutes, to masturbate over her.

When the body got too discomposed,
I'd just jack off, letting it fall on her . . .
—It sounds crazy, but I tell you
sometimes it was beautiful—; I don't know how
to say it, but for a minute, everything was possible—;

As she decomposes, "more and more of the skull" shows through. Herbert White notices that "the nights became clearer, and the buds,—erect, like nipples . . ." The poet's eye slips in and gifts his monster with an erotic clarity that such monsters likely don't possess in real life.

Whenever I read this poem, I want an antidote. Herbert White is most disrupting when poet and murderer become one, speaking in the same expulsive voice: "I wanted to see beneath it, cut / beneath it, and make it / somehow, come alive . . ." It is not a sanitization, exactly—after all, the narrator ends up in a hell of self-loathing. But it stands in a long line of dead-girl begats, if I can call them that, where eros erupts from the demolishment of women.

In the time of #metoo that Harvey Weinstein ushered in, a time when everything from Balthus's *Thérèse Dreaming* to the standards for *The Paris Review* are being reevaluated, it's utterly bracing to find two new books of poetry by women that let the girls speak—speak like Cassandra, speak like Scheherazade, and by speaking, not die.

Curiously, both are by women poets rooted in a sense of place—and that place is Virginia, where they grew up—its woods, rivers, and fields. The first, Molly McCully Brown's *The Virginia State Colony for Epileptics and Feebleminded,* gives a steady, unapologetic, almost liturgical voice to fictive priests, caregivers, and patients from a century ago in a real-life residential hospital in Virginia that housed and sterilized thousands of patients. It's a quiet knockout of a book in which the voices of the broken, deformed girls are unforgettable.

In the opening poem, "The Central Virginia Training Center" Brown refers obliquely to her own real-life cerebral palsy, describing her "spastic, palsied and off-balance" body, which by "an accident of luck or grace" escaped a place that could have imprisoned her a half century earlier. But her body has brought her close enough to feel what it must have been like: "I'm taking crooked notes about this place . . . I am my own kind of damaged there." From those notes flow girls whose voices exhume and empower them. They have been sterilized, adding worthlessness to worthlessness:

I will remember this day as the day
I was cleaved from my body.
Whatever they did, I am

the silt that slips between your fingers
when you dredge for the bright things
at the bottom of a pond.

These are girls (never women) defined by uselessness, since their wrecked bodies cannot reproduce—"useless approximations of live things, littered on the beds" and "a useless barge lit up, bearing away on the water." They can, merely by their existence, destroy faith: "we are a whole host of reasons / to stop believing in anything." But they also move like a stately procession of quiet Furies through Brown's clear, cadenced lines—and miraculously reclaim life. These girls are perfectly capable of describing unspeakable acts of abuse and molestation. In the boarded up "blindroom" where one can be left tied up for days:

Sometimes, someone follows you in,
Puts his hands around your throat.

But we are not abandoned there, with the brute act—a man who is "hot and oversweet above you." A crack in the window boards lets in a sliver of light, just enough for redemption, starting with each finger of an illumined hand:

. . . think
about each finger & think
about the sky until
it happened.

Think about your body.
Think about infinity.
Think about God.

The blindroom is "the worst place you've ever been" and is also "the world before God made it."

These are girls who can transubstantiate, who while tied up on floorboards and raped in a boarded-up room can touch infinity and God. It is an extraordinary act of rehabilitation.

As spare and compassionate as Brown's voice is, Heather Derr-Smith's poems in *Thrust* uncoil wildly from the page like Medusa hair. The title of this book is a declamation and an act of possession. Here, too, violence against women is transformed into song, transubstantiated into love. These girls—who are punched, raped, terrorized, left for dead—never truly submit:

One boy pushed her down in the honeysuckle
And tried to fuck her, but she punched him off, jab

to the neck, her palm facing the ground.

And then moments later, transformation:
The girl's hair lifted like veins—

not biblical, not evangelical, but something primitive
and voodoo, Made of stardust. Made of dirt.

Made of slut.

Derr-Smith's poesy is lush, in-love, often lapidary, and deeply unafraid. Her book is replete with "the punch that breaks the jaw in piece / the hit that leaves you speechless"; the girl who is "hit again when she ducks. / So her dad kicks her down the hall." And she offers the battered girl's timeless conflation of hurt with love: "I know one thing. / I was worth beating down, a pulp. Someone *wanted* me so damn bad."

In Derr-Smith's woods, dead girls are not merely erotic and decomposing mannequins. They give rise to pink teeth and vexing questions:

When I left my father's house I came to the place where the girls were found:

Pink teeth, indicate possible violence, quick oxidation of hemoglobin
or possible strangulation
remains found near water, no obvious taste of salt.
That's what they said: *no obvious taste.* What I want to know is
who tasted?

The query—with its tinge of appalled disbelief—seems a line that only a woman would need, and be willing, to ask. The reader inevitably pauses uneasily after that question—and in that pause is writ a whole history of misogyny and its sanitization.

But violence is the beginning of reclamation. An "esophageal tunnel of woods" prefigures the transformation of the female walking in them. She hears "the wilderness ad libbing its prayers in the whippoorwill and the cypress." She answers with her own song: "*Ad libitum*, according to my desire." That song is a psalm to "the you that sprang from my guts every time I was hit or kicked / green bruises like the leaves in the boughs / The you of my being I imagined beautiful out of the penetralia / of that molt self." She rises "from the blows, / like the ring of a bell, unbreakable." She is: "phantasmagorical, huge, oracle" and veers "away from danger / in a sudden thrust of beauty."

The thrust is hers, and the beauty is everywhere. It is in the hymnal choir of her language—"spangled with moss and the acapella of crickets." It flows in delicious homages to boys, their "bodies of pure delight" and "the boys, the boys / swinging like a pendulum in the blooms." It is evident in the speaker's own desire, which reduces her to an "awestruck thing at the steps / of your pelvis." She is as vulnerable as any woman, but she claims it in the name of love: her body and her eye are a "hymen" that is "lancinated" by a man's beauty. She becomes supernatural, her bones artillery: "The woman levitated over Barcelona / She had a rifle for a clavicle."

It is a riven world, where a boy can promise *"I'm here for you"* and yet one's own father can call at three a.m.: *"You slut, you're a slut just like your mother."* But she embraces it all:

> The morning before I met you,
> a homeless man followed me down the street
> saying, *Come here you cunt. I'm going to kill you.*
> But when you asked me how I was,
> I said *good*, like God in the beginning declaring all things good

"it was good" says Herbert White of hitting a girl on the head. "I said *good*," counters Derr-Smith's narrator, anointing the world. White's "good" is built on a desire to annihilate that is writ into the entire history of our species. Derr-Smith's "good" is full of supernumerary blessing, so vast it likens itself to the divine. It is, indeed, the necessary antidote at the right time.

Neither of these books seek retribution, unlike Sylvia Plath's Lady Lazarus, who eats men like air. Instead, they fashion wholeness from (and in spite of) a fabric of daily transgression and harm. From both poets, these are necessary gifts in a time of reckoning for women everywhere.

CONTRIBUTOR NOTES

Ljubica Arsovska is editor-in-chief of the long-established Skopje cultural magazine *Kulturen Život* and a distinguished literary translator from English into Macedonian, and vice versa. Her translations from English into Macedonian include books by Isaiah Berlin, Toni Morrison, Susan Sontag, and plays of Lope De Vega, Harold Pinter, Edward Albee, Tom Stoppard, and Tennessee Williams. Her translations from Macedonian into English include works by Lidija Dimkovska, Dejan Dukovski, Tomislav Osmanli, Ilija Petrushevski, Sotir Golabovski, Dimitar Bashevski, Radovan Pavlovski, Gordana Mihailova Boshnakoska, Katica Kulafkova, and Liljana Dirjan, among others.

Jennifer Buentello is a writer, teacher, and translator. She serves as managing editor of *Iron Horse Literary Review*. Her stories, essays, and translations have appeared or are forthcoming in *Florida Review, Denver Quarterly, Texas Review, Los Angeles Review, Newfound,* and elsewhere. Jennifer currently pursues her PhD at Texas Tech University.

Marcelo Hernandez Castillo is the author of the award-winning poetry collections *Cenzontle* (BOA Editions), *Dulce* (Northwestern University Press), and his most recent book is *Children of the Land: A Memoir (*Harper Collins). A founding member of the Undocupoets Campaign, he was the first undocumented student to graduate from the Helen Zell Writers Program at the University of Michigan. He lives in Northern California with his wife and son where he teaches poetry to incarcerated youth and also teaches at the Ashland University Low-Res MFA program.

Rebecca Childers, a West Virginia native, has an MFA from West Virginia University. She teaches writing and film at Marshall University, and she lives with her border collie named Chuck.

Tiana Clark is the author of *Equilibrium* (Bull City Press, 2016). Her first full-length collection, *I Can't Talk About the Trees Without the Blood* (University of Pittsburgh Press, 2018), won the 2017 Agnes Lynch Starrett Prize. Her writing has appeared in or is forthcoming from the *New Yorker, Kenyon Review, American Poetry Review,* and elsewhere.

Katharine Coldiron's work has appeared in *Ms., The Rumpus,* the *Collagist, Entropy,* and elsewhere. She lives in California and blogs at the *Fictator.*

Oliver de la Paz is the author of five books of poetry. His latest book, *The Boy in the Labyrinth,* was published by the University of Akron Press in 2019. A founding member of Kundiman, he chairs the advisory board and teaches at the College of the Holy Cross and in the Low-Res program at PLU.

Lidija Dimkovska (b.1971, Skopje, Macedonia) has published six books of poetry and three novels, awarded and translated in more than twenty languages. In the States, in 2006, Ugly Duckling Presse from New York published her first collection of poetry in English, *Do Not Awaken Them with Hammers.* In 2012, Copper Canyon Press published her second book of poetry *pH Neutral History* (short-listed for the Best Translated Book Award 2013), and in 2016, Two Lines Press published her novel *A Spare Life* (long-listed for the Best Translated Book Award 2017).

Dara Yen Elerath received her MFA in poetry from the Institute of American Indian Arts. Her first book, *The Dark Braid,* won the twentieth John Ciardi Prize for Poetry and is forthcoming in 2020. Her poems have appeared in the *American Poetry Review, AGNI, Plume, Poet Lore, Superstition Review* and elsewhere. She resides in Albuquerque, New Mexico, where she writes and designs.

Carl-Christian Elze, born in 1974, lives in Leipzig and writes poems, short stories and plays. He studied biology and German studies at the University of Leipzig, and later creative writing at the *Deutsche Literaturinstitut Leipzig.* Recent awards for his work include the Joachim-Ringelnatz Prize (2015) and residencies at the Künstlerhaus Edenkoben (2017) and the Deutsche Studienzentrum in Venice (2016), where he wrote the poems for his 2019 book *lang-*

sames ermatten im labyrinth. Other recent books include, *diese kleinen, in der luft hängenden, bergpredigenden gebilde: poems* (Verlagshaus Berlin, 2016), and *Oda und der ausgestopfte Vater* (kreuzerbooks, 2018), a book of short stories about growing up with the animals at the Leipzig Zoo where his father was head veterinarian. Elze is a member of the German PEN Center.

Malva Flores is author, among others, of the following books: *Galápagos* (Era, 2016); *La culpa es por cantar. Apuntes sobre poesía y poetas de hoy* [The fault is for singing. Notes on poetry and poets today] (Literal Publishing / Conaculta, 2014); *Aparece un instante, Nevermore* [Appears for an instant, Nevermore] (Bonobos / UNAM, 2012), *Viaje de Vuelta. Estampas de una revista* [Journey of Return. Prints from a magazine] (FCE, 2011), *Luz de la Materia* [Light of Matter] (ERA, 2010), Passage of the Tree (Literal Publishing, 2006), *Malparaíso* [Bad paradise] (Eldorado, 2003), *Casa nómada* [Nomadic house] (Joaquín Mortiz, 1999), *Ladera de las cosas vivas* [Hillside of living things] (CNCA, 1997), *Pasión de caza* [Passion of hunting] (Gob. Del Estado de Jalisco, 1993). In 2006, Flores won the José Revueltas National Essay Prize with her book *El ocaso de los poetas intelectuales* [The Twilight of the Intellectual Poet] (UV, 2010). In 1999, she received the Aguascalientes National Poetry Prize, and in 1991, she also received the Elías Nandino National Young Poetry Prize. Her poetry has been translated into English, Portuguese, Japanese, German, and Dutch.

kwabena foli was born in Belgium but raised in the Southside of Chicago. Current and forthcoming publications include *Mikrokosmos Journal, Meridian, Crab Orchard Review, Cream City Review, Salt Hill Journal*, and elsewhere. His work is also anthologized in *Revise the Psalm: Work Celebrating the Writing of Gwendolyn Brooks* from Curbside Press. He's a member of Nu-Being Collective and was a resident at Banff Centre of Arts, Poetry Center of Chicago, and Chicago Artist Coalition. He currently lives in Chicago.

Adam Gnuse's debut novel, *Girl in the Walls*, will be published in 2021 by Ecco & Fourth Estate. A former *Kenyon Review* Peter Taylor fellow, Adam earned his MFA from UNC Wilmington, and his short stories have appeared in *New South, Passages North, Potomac Review*, and other journals. More information is available at adamgnuse.com.

Joanna Rafael Goldberg is a former New Yorker and Angeleno currently living and writing in London. Her work can be found in *Bomb, Partisan Hotel, Expat Press*, and *Queen Mob's Tea House*. www.joannarafaelgoldberg.com

Mario J. Gonzales was born and raised in Parlier, CA, a small agricultural town outside of Fresno. His grandparents left Mexico in the early 1900s, refugees of the Mexican revolution and settled in central California. He has a PhD in cultural anthropology from Washington State University and currently works as an anthropology professor at New Mexico Highlands University. His short fiction can be found in the *New England Review, Quarterly West, Sonora Review, Blue Mesa Review*, and other literary journals. He has a short story collection entitled *Descanos*, which he hopes to publish soon.

James Hoch's books are *Miscreants* and *A Parade of Hands. Last Pawn Shop in New Jersey* is due in 2022 from LSU press. His poems have appeared in *POETRY, The New Republic, Washington Post, Slate, Chronicle Review of Higher Education, American Poetry Review, New England Review, Kenyon Review, Tin House, Ploughshares, Virginia Quarterly Review* and many other magazines, and has been selected for inclusion in *Best American Poetry 2019*. He has received fellowships from the NEA, Bread Loaf and Sewanee writer's conferences, St. Albans School for Boys, The Frost Place and Summer Literary Seminars. Currently, he is Professor of Creative Writing at Ramapo College of NJ and Guest Faculty at Sarah Lawrence.

Pete Hsu is a Taiwanese American writer in Los Angeles. His work has been featured in the *Los Angeles Review of Books, F(r)iction, The Bare Life Review*, and others. He was a 2017 PEN America Emerging Voices Fellow and is the current fiction editor for *Angels Flight • literary west*.

Recently retired after thirty years of teaching at Western Wyoming College, poet and essayist **Rick Kempa** is free to pursue his twin passions of writing and walking. *Too Vast for Sleep*, his third book of poems, was recently published by Littoral Press. He is the founding editor of the literary journal *Deep Wild: Writing from the Backcountry.* www.rickkempa.com

David Keplinger is the author of six collections of poetry, including *The Long Answer: New and Selected* (2020), and *Another City* (2018), which was awarded the 2019 UNT Rilke Prize. He teaches at American University in Washington DC.

Sophie Klahr is the author of *Meet Me Here At Dawn* (YesYes Books, 2016) and the chapbook_____ *Versus Recovery* (Pilot Books, 2007). Her poetry appears in the *New Yorker, American Poetry Review, Ploughshares, AGNI,* and other publications. She lives mostly in California and Nebraska.

Joe Paul Kroll is a freelance translator and editor based in Wiesbaden, Germany. jpkroll.wixsite.com/home

Keetje Kuipers's third collection, *All Its Charms,* was published by BOA Editions in 2019. Her poems have appeared widely, including in the *New York Times Magazine,* as well as the *Pushcart Prize* and *Best American Poetry* anthologies. Previously a Wallace Stegner fellow, Bread Loaf fellow, and the Margery Davis Boyden Wilderness Writing Resident, Kuipers is currently Editor of *Poetry Northwest.*

Rhonda Lancaster holds an MA in creative writing and literature from Fairleigh Dickinson University. She is president of Project Write, Inc., leading workshops for young writers include the first-of-its-kind Young Screenwriters' Conference. She teaches English and creative writing for high school students and college composition courses in Winchester, VA. Her writing has appeared in the *Los Angeles Review, Disability Experiences* (Gale), and *Anthology of Appa-*

lachian Writers (Vols. VI & VII). She is a member of WV Writers Inc. She lives with her husband and three dogs in Capon Bridge, West Virginia.

Anna Leahy is the author of the nonfiction book *Tumor* and the poetry collections *Aperture* and *Constituents of Matter*. Her essays and poetry have appeared at *Aeon*, *The Atlantic*, *BuzzFeed*, *Crab Orchard Review*, *Fifth Wednesday Journal*, *LitHub*, *The Southern Review*, *The Pinch*, *The Rumpus*, and elsewhere, and her essays have won top awards from the *Los Angeles Review*, *Ninth Letter*, and *Dogwood*. She directs the MFA in Creative Writing program at Chapman University, where she edits the international journal *TAB* and curates the Tabula Poetica reading series. See more at www.amleahy.com.

Mia Ayumi Malhotra is the author of *Isako Isako* (Alice James Books, 2019), winner of the 2017 Alice James Award. She received her MFA from the University of Washington and is a Kundiman and VONA/Voices Fellow. Her poems have appeared in *Greensboro Review*, *Drunken Boat*, *Best New Poets*, and elsewhere. She currently lives in the San Francisco Bay Area.

John Mattson is a writer, screenwriter, songwriter, and teacher. He lives in Los Angeles with his wife and son. His bio is incomplete.

Helena Mesa is the author of *Horse Dance Underwater* and a co-editor for *Mentor & Muse: Essays from Poets to Poets*. She teaches at Albion College.

Wayne Miller is the author of five poetry collections, including *Post-* (Milkweed, 2016), which won the UNT Rilke Prize and the Colorado Book Award, and *We the Jury*, which Milkweed will publish in 2021. He teaches at the University of Colorado Denver and serves as editor/managing editor of *Copper Nickel*.

Michaela Maria Müller was born in Dachau, Germany. She is a novelist and journalist. She studied history at the Humboldt University of Berlin. She is currently working as a journalist and reporter for *Sueddeutsche Zeitung, Die Zeit, Die Tageszeitung*. Her latest book, *Auf See. Die Geschichte von Ayan und Samir*, appeared 2016. She is a fellow of the Bavarian Academy of Writing and a former resident at the Franz-Edelmaier-Residency of the Swiss Society for the European Convention on Human Rights (2019). https://www.michaelamariamueller.de

John Murillo is the author of the poetry collections, *Up Jump the Boogie* (Cypher 2010), finalist for both the Kate Tufts Discovery Award and the PEN Open Book Award, and *Kontemporary Amerikan Poetry* (forthcoming from Four Way Books 2020). His honors include a Pushcart Prize, the J. Howard and Barbara M.J. Wood Prize from the Poetry Foundation, and fellowships from the National Endowment for the Arts, the Bread Loaf Writers Conference, Fine Arts Work Center in Provincetown, Cave Canem Foundation, and the Wisconsin Institute for Creative Writing. His work has appeared in *Ploughshares, Poetry, Prairie Schooner*, and *Best American Poetry 2017*. He is an assistant professor of English at Wesleyan University and also teaches in the low residency MFA program at Sierra Nevada College.

Jim Natal is the multi-year Pushcart Prize-nominated author of two collections of poems in haibun form, *52 Views: The Haibun Variations* and *Spare Room*, as well as three previous lyric collections, including *Memory and Rain*. His work has appeared in many journals and anthologies, including *Hayden's Ferry Review, San Pedro River Review, Hotel Amerika, Angle of Reflection*, and *Los Angeles in the 1970s*. He is the director of The Literary Southwest Poetry series and co-founder of Conflux Press.

Gillian (Jill) Neimark is an author of adult and children's fiction and nonfiction. A former contributing editor at *Discover Magazine*, she has also written for *Scientific American, Science, Nautilus, Aeon*, the *New York Times, NPR, Quartz*, and *Psychology Today*. Her novel, *Bloodsong*, was published in hardcover in 1993 and paperback in 1994, was a BOMC selection, translated into Italian, German and Hebrew, and optioned for film. She is the author of three picture books and two middle-grade novels, and her poetry has been published in the *Cimarron Review*, *Borderlands*, the *Massachusetts Review*, and the *Columbia Review*.

LJ Pemberton is a writer / artist / futurist and the founder of StoryWoolf. Her stories, essays, and poetry have been featured in *PANK*, the *Electric Encyclopedia of Experimental Literature*, *Hobart*, *VICE*, the *Brooklyn Rail*, and elsewhere. She has an MFA from Columbia University and is formerly an assistant editor at *NOON*.

Maya Pindyck's latest poetry collection, *Emoticoncert*, was published by Four Way Books in 2016. Raised in Massachusetts and Tel Aviv, she lives in Brooklyn, NY.

Meghann Plunkett is a poet and screenwriter. She is the recipient of the *Missouri Review*'s Editors' Prize as well as the *Third Coast Magazine* Poetry Prize. Her work can be found in *Best New Poets 2018*, *Narrative Magazine*, *Washington Square Review*, among others. Since serving as the Poetry Reader for *The New Yorker*, she can be found screenwriting for Shondaland's TV shows *Grey's Anatomy* and *Station 19*. Visit her at meghannplunkett.com

Caroline Wilcox Reul is a freelance lexicographer and translator, with an MA in computational linguistics and German language and literature from the Ludwig-Maximilians-Universität in Munich. She is the translator of *Wer lebt / Who Lives* by Elisabeth Borchers (Tavern Books, 2017), the co-editor of the poetry anthology, *Over Land and Rising* (9 Bridges, 2017), and the current poetry editor for the *Timberline Review*. She was awarded the Summer/Fall 2018 Gabo Prize for Literature in Translation and Multilingual Texts. Her work has appeared or is forthcoming in the *PEN Poetry Series*, the *Broadsided Press*, *Tupelo Quarterly*, *Poetry International*, *Lyrikline.org*, and *Lunch Ticket*.

Liana Sakelliou was born in Athens where she studied English literature at the University of Athens and did postgraduate studies in Edinburgh, in Essex

(UK) and at Pennsylvania State University. Since 1999, she has been a professor of American literature, specializing in contemporary poetry and creative writing in the Department of English Language and Literature of the University of Athens. She has received scholarships from the Fulbright Foundation, the Department of Hellenic Studies of Princeton University, the University of Coimbra and the British Council for her academic and writing activities, and a translation award in 2014 for her book on Emily Dickinson. She has published sixteen books, as well as numerous articles, poems, book reviews and translations in Greek and American periodicals. Her poems have been translated into several languages.

Born in Nevada and raised in California, **Don Schofield** left America in 1980. Since that time, he has been living and writing in Greece, traveling extensively, teaching and serving as an administrator at various universities—Greek, American and British—in Athens and Thessaloniki. Fluent in Greek, a citizen of both his homeland and his adopted country (or, more precisely, the country that adopted him), he has published several poetry collections, as well as an anthology of American poets in Greece and translations of contemporary Greek poets. He has been awarded the Allen Ginsberg Award (US), the John D. Criticos Prize (UK) and a Stanley J. Seeger Writer-in-Residence fellowship at Princeton University. His first book, *Approximately Paradise*, was a finalist for the Walt Whitman Award, and his translations have been nominated for a Pushcart Prize and the Greek National Translation Award. Recently retired, he and his companion, Aleka, live in both Athens and Thessaloniki.

Corinna McClanahan Schroeder is the author of the poetry collection *Inked*, winner of the 2014 X. J. Kennedy Poetry Prize. Her poems have recently appeared in such journals as *Blackbird*, *Gulf Coast*, and *The Southern Review*. She lives in Los Angeles and teaches in the Writing Program at the University of Southern California.

Yente Serdatsky was born in 1877 in a shtetl near Kovne, Lithuania, and died

May 1, 1962, in New York. She began writing in 1905, when she abandoned her husband and three children and moved to Warsaw; however, the family reunited by the time they moved to Chicago in 1907. She was known during her lifetime as a rabble-rouser who repeatedly lost her income by feuding with other writers and editors. Many of her stories focused on the frustrations of countless Jewish women during the turn of the century, a time of pogroms and economic depression in the Pale, mass Jewish immigration to the US, a breakdown in traditional family structures, and so-called liberatory leftist politics heralded by men who remained committed sexists. Eventually, in 1922, a feud with Abe Cahan, the editor of the famed *Forverts*, left her without a venue for her fiction. She did not write again until 1949, when she began to compose short stories, along with comedic epistolary and accounts of her life—writing that today might be labelled creative nonfiction.

Rochelle Spencer is author of *AfroSurrealism: The African Diaspora's Surrealist Fiction* (Routledge, 2019) and co-editor, with Jina Ortiz, of *All About Skin: Short Fiction by Women of Color* (University of Wisconsin Press, 2014). Rochelle is a former board member of the Hurston Wright Foundation and a current member of the National Book Critics Circle and AICA. Her work has appeared in *Lithub, Mosaic, The Millions, Poets & Writers, Callaloo*, the *African American Review, Los Angeles Review, Women's Review of Books*, the *Gay and Lesbian Review*, and other publications.

Patricia Marsh Stefanovska is a linguist with an MA in General Linguistics from the University of Manchester. She is also a writer of fiction and nonfiction, author of *The Scribe of the Soul* and *The Enigma of the Margate Shell Grotto*, and translator of a number of plays and poems from Macedonian into English. She lectured in English at the University of Skopje for a long period before returning to live and work in the UK in 1992.

Susan Thurston is a novelist, journalist, and award-winning poet with work appearing in publications including *The Writer's Almanac* and *Low Down and*

Coming On (Red Dragonfly Press). Her novel *Sister of Grendel* (The Black Hat Press) came out in 2016. A passionate cook, she co-authored *Cooking Up the Good Life* with Chef Jenny Breen (University of Minnesota Press).

Corey Van Landingham is the author of *Antidote* and *Love Letter to Who Owns the Heavens*, forthcoming from Tupelo Press. She is the recipient of a National Endowment for the Arts Fellowship and a Wallace Stegner Fellowship from Stanford University, and teaches at the University of Illinois.

Cady Vishniac works as a medical editor in Ann Arbor, Michigan. Her fiction has been published in *Glimmer Train* and *New England Review*, and won the anthology prize at *New Stories from the Midwest*. This is her first work of published translation, finished during a fellowship at the Yiddish Book Center in Amherst, Massachusetts.

Claire Wahmanholm is the author of *Wilder*, winner of the 2018 Lindquist & Vennum Prize for Poetry (forthcoming from Milkweed Editions this November). Her work has appeared in *DIAGRAM*, *The Journal*, *PANK*, *Bennington Review*, the *Kenyon Review* (online), *New Poetry from the Midwest 2017*, and elsewhere. She lives in the Twin Cities.

Jennifer Wheelock is a poet and painter living in Los Angeles. Her poems have appeared or are forthcoming in many print and digital journals and anthologies, including *Feminine Collective*, *Post Road*, *Lake Effect*, *Flycatcher*, *Diagram*, *River Styx*, *Atlanta Review*, and *The Inflectionist Review*. She works at UCLA.

Shannon K. Winston's poems have or will appear in *RHINO*, *Crab Creek Review*, and *SWWIM Every Day*, among others. Her work has been nominated for a Pushcart Prize and several times for the Best of the Net. She earned her MFA at Warren Wilson College. Find her here: https://shannonkwinston.com/

CONJUNCTIONS

biannual print and e-book volumes

weekly online magazine

art: "bond" by amy guidry

cream city review

www.creamcityreview.org • est. 1975

submit jan 1 - apr 1

fiction • nonfiction • poetry • art